'When I said list of what needs to be done I expected a page or two—not a doctoral thesis.'

Willa shrugged. 'What can I say? I'm an over-achiever and it was fun…putting my brain and my training to work.'

Rob tapped the folder and held her eyes. 'Good job, Willa. I'm seriously impressed.'

Willa sucked in her breath, hope shining from her eyes. 'Impressed enough to give me the job?'

Rob, hoping that he wasn't making a huge mistake, slowly nodded. 'Yeah. I'm handing the paperwork over to you.'

Willa shot up so fast that she skidded backwards over the polished wooden floor and did a crazy dance on the spot. 'Yes! Yes, yes, yes, *yes*!'

Rob tensed as a bundle of warm, fragrant flesh fell into his lap. She was going to complicate this…he could just tell.

SYDNEY'S MOST ELIGIBLE...

The men everyone *is talking about!*

Young, rich and gorgeous, Rob, Scott, Brodie
and Luke have the world at their feet
and women queuing to get between their sheets.

Find out how the past and the present collide for them
in this stylish, sexy and glamorous new quartet!

These sexy Sydney tycoons didn't get to the top by
taking the easy way—the only thing they love more
than a challenge is a woman who knows her mind!

So let the fireworks begin…!

HER BOSS BY DAY…
by Joss Wood
Available January 2015

THE MILLIONAIRE'S PROPOSITION
by Avril Tremayne
Available February 2015

THE TYCOON'S STOWAWAY
by Stefanie London
Available March 2015

THE HOTEL MAGNATE'S DEMAND
by Jennifer Rae
Available April 2015

You won't want to miss any of the fabulous books
in this sizzling mini-series!

HER BOSS BY DAY...

BY
JOSS WOOD

Published in Great Britain 2015
by Mills & Boon, an imprint of Harlequin (UK) Limited,
Eton House, 18-24 Paradise Road, Richmond, Surrey, TW9 1SR

© 2015 Harlequin Books S.A.

Special thanks and acknowledgement are given to Joss Wood
for her contribution to the *Sydney's Most Eligible...* series.

ISBN: 978-0-263-24832-6

Printed and bound in Spain
by Blackprint CPI, Barcelona

Joss Wood wrote her first book at the age of eight and has never really stopped. Her passion for putting letters on a blank screen is matched only by her love of books and travelling—especially to the wild places of Southern Africa—and possibly by her hatred of ironing and making school lunches.

Fuelled by coffee, when she's not writing or being a hands-on mum Joss, with her background in business and marketing, works for a non-profit organisation to promote the local economic development and collective business interests of the area where she resides. Happily and chaotically surrounded by books, family and friends, she lives in Kwa-Zulu Natal, South Africa, with her husband, children and their many pets.

Other Modern Tempted™ titles by Joss Wood:

YOUR BED OR MINE?
MORE THAN A FLING?
FLIRTING WITH THE FORBIDDEN
THE LAST GUY SHE SHOULD CALL

For my sister, Jen Seymour-Blight,
who lives far too far away in Australia. Miss you.

CHAPTER ONE

'You will not get me into bed tonight. Tomorrow night isn't looking good for you, either.'

In the huge bathroom mirror of the upmarket Saints restaurant in Surry Hills, Willa Moore-Fisher practised the phrase and shook her head in disgust. She was being too nice and her sleazy blind date didn't deserve that much consideration. Obtuse to a fault, he might think that there was a chance of sleeping with her in the future. Which there wasn't—ever. She'd rather gouge her eye out with a blunt twig.

'I'd explain why I think you're an arrogant jerk, but then your brain would explode from you trying to understand.' Willa tested the words out loud.

And wasn't that an image to make her smile? *Ka-boom!* She could just imagine that smirking, arrogant expression blown apart by the suitable application of high-impact explosives. There were, she decided, very few personal problems that couldn't be solved by a little C4.

Willa imagined that the explosive would work really well on soon-to-be-ex-husbands too...

Maybe you should just go back in there and give him another chance, suggested nice Willa, doormat Willa. *It might be that this disastrous date is your fault; if you were a little better at drawing him out, at asking the right questions, at being more interesting...*

Wild Willa dropped doormat Willa with a snappy kick to her temple. *That's what you did for eight years, moron; you tried to bring the best out in Wayne, tried to change yourself so that he would change. And how did that work out for you?*

'Catch a freakin' clue, dumbass.' Willa pointed a finger at her reflection. 'Find your balls, metaphorically speaking, tell him he's wasting your time and get the hell out of here.'

Yeah, like you'd ever actually say that aloud, taunted wild Willa. *You're the world's biggest wuss and you'd rather put up with someone's crap than take the chance of making anyone mad at you.*

Maybe some day she'd learn to stand up for herself.

Wild Willa just snorted her disbelief.

God, these voices in her head exhausted her.

'So, is this talking to yourself something new or did you always do it and I didn't notice?'

In the mirror Willa saw the slick blonde and admired her exquisitely cut and coloured short, smooth bob. Then she clocked the mischievous tawny-brown eyes and spun around in shock.

'Amy? My God, *Amy*!'

'Hey Willa.'

Amy walked towards her on spiked heels. Her shift dress showed off her curves and her make-up and salon-perfect hair were flawless. Willa scanned her face and there, in the tilt of her mouth and in the humour dancing in her eyes, she saw her best friend at eighteen—the mischievous flirt who, just by being Amy, had opened up a world of fun to her that summer so long ago.

'Amy. My God…what are you doing here?'

Willa leaned in for a hug and was surprised by the fact that she didn't want to let Amy go. Why had she *ever* let her go? Let her fade from her life? That summer in the Whitsundays, their core group of friends—Amy, Brodie, Scott, Chantal, her older brother Luke—had been her world and, like so much else, she'd given them up when she married Wayne.

Stupid girl.

'Having dinner with my flatmate before we go clubbing,' Amy replied, keeping hold of Willa's hand. 'But you—why are you talking to yourself?'

'Short answer…an excruciatingly bad blind date that I am trying to get out of.' Willa tipped her head to the bathroom window. 'Do you think I'm skinny enough to slip through there?'

Amy looked her up and down. 'Actually, you are far too skinny—and back up. What about Wayne? You married him, didn't you?'

Willa lifted her ringless left hand. 'About to be divorced. That was a…mistake.'

Hmm…a mistake. That was a major understatement, but she'd go with it.

Amy pursed her lips. 'I'm sorry… God, Willa, so much time has passed. We need to catch up. *Now.*'

'What about my date and your friend?' Willa asked. She had already been in the bathroom for an inexcusably long time—she was being so rude.

So what? Wild Willa rolled her eyes.

'*Pfft*…your date sounds like a moron and Jessica was exchanging hot looks with a guy across the room. She won't miss me.'

Amy stalked to the door, yanked it open and let out one of her high-pitched, loud and distinctive whistles. Willa wasn't surprised when she soon saw a Saints waiter outside the door.

'Is the small function room empty?' Amy asked.

'Yes, ma'am.'

'Good. Tell Guido that I'm using it for a while, and ask him to please bring me a bottle of that Burnt Tree Chardonnay I like and put it on my tab,' ordered Amy, and with a luscious smile sent him on his way.

The kid, drooling, whirled away to do the goddess's bidding. It seemed that Amy, always a good flirt, now had a PhD in getting men to jump through her hoops.

Amy turned back to Willa and shrugged at her astounded expression. 'I hold a lot of work functions here. Guido owes me.'

Amy led Willa out of the bathroom, down a decorated passage and into a small function room that held a boardroom table at one end and a cluster of chairs at the other. She pulled Willa to the set of wingback chairs and gestured to her to sit.

'It's so good to see you, Willa,' Amy said, taking the seat opposite her. 'You look so…different. Classy…rich.'

Willa knew what she saw: it was the same face and body she looked at every day. She was still the same height, taller than most woman but skinnier than she'd been at eighteen. Thick, mocha and auburn shoulder-length hair, with a heavy fringe surrounding a pixie face dominated by silver-green eyes.

'That's because I *am* classy…and my husband—ex—whatever—is rich,' Willa said, making a conscious effort to keep the bitterness from her voice but doubting that she'd succeeded. 'Gym, designer clothes, best hairdresser in Sydney.'

Amy lightly touched her knee. 'Was it awful…being married to him?'

Willa considered lying, thought about glossing over the truth, but then she saw the understanding and sympathy in Amy's eyes and realised that while she wouldn't tell Amy— tell *anyone*—the whole truth, she didn't have to blatantly lie. She and Amy had been through too much for her to lie.

'Not awful, no. Boring—absolutely. Wayne wanted a young, gorgeous trophy wife, and that's what I've been for the past eight years.'

An eight-year marriage condensed into two sentences…

'God, a trophy wife.' Amy winced. 'But you're so damn

bright…you always wanted to study accountancy, economics, business.'

'Yeah, well, Wayne wanted beauty and acquiescence, not brains. I kept up with the markets, trends, but he'd didn't like his wife talking business. I was supposed to be seen and not heard.'

'I always thought that he was waste of space.'

At the knock on the door Amy got up to accept a bottle and glasses, thanked the waiter profusely and adeptly poured them both a glass.

Amy took a sip of her wine and took her seat again. 'Why do I get the feeling that I'm getting the sanitised version here?'

Because she wasn't a fool. 'My dead marriage is a very boring topic, Amy.'

'You were never boring, Willa. Quiet, maybe—intense, shy. Not boring. And I know that you probably gave Wayne-the-Pain a hundred and fifty per cent because the Willa I knew bent over backwards to make everyone happy. When you make a promise or a decision it takes a nuclear bomb to dislodge you.'

'I'm not that bad,' Willa protested, though she knew she was. She didn't give up—or in—easily.

'You hate going against your word.' Amy sent her a strange, sad smile. 'You were distraught that you had to ask Luke for help that night in the Whitsundays because I'd begged you not to.'

Willa bit her lip, still seeing Amy, battered and bloody, tears and crimson sand on her face. Her black and blue eye and her split cheek from fighting off Justin's unwelcome advances on the beach. Sometimes she still saw her face in her dreams and woke up in a cold sweat.

'I'm sorry, but I needed Luke to help me to help you.'

Amy looked into her wine glass. 'I know…it's okay. It was all a long time ago. How *is* Luke?'

There was an odd tremor in her voice which Willa instantly picked up. Amy and Luke had always had some sort of love-hate, weird reaction to each other that Willa could never quite put her finger on.

'He's fine…still single, still driven. He's working on a massive hotel development in Singapore—the biggest of his career.'

Amy eventually raised her eyes to meet Willa's. 'Are you still in contact with the others from the resort? Brodie, Chantal, Scott?'

Willa shrugged. 'Loosely, via social media and the very occasional e-mail. Chantal is still dancing, Scott is one of the city's most brilliant young architects, and Brodie is the heart and soul of a company that runs luxury yacht tours down the Gold Coast. I haven't seen them or socialised with them….nothing has been the same since the week you and Brodie left.'

Happy to be off the subject of her dysfunctional marriage, Willa cast her mind back to that summer they'd spent in the Whitsundays, when a group of strangers had arrived at the very fancy Weeping Reef resort, ready and rocking to start a holiday season of working all day and having fun all night.

It still amazed her that the five of them—six if she included Luke—had clicked so well. They were such a mixed bag of personalities.

They'd laughed and loved and drunk and partied, and then laughed and loved and partied some more. They'd been really good at it, and the first two months of their summer holiday had flown past. Then their idyll had been shattered when two dreadful incidents had dumped a bucket of angst and recrimination and guilt over their magical interlude and ripped their clique apart.

And set Willa on a path that she now deeply regretted.

'To go back a whole bunch of steps—we were talking

about you and Wayne and what caused the split,' Amy said, pulling her back to their conversation. She refilled their glasses and lifted an eyebrow.

'Oh...that.'

'Yes, that.'

How strange it was that after so long she and Amy could just fall into conversation as if it was yesterday... how strange and how right.

In the natural order of things they shouldn't have been friends... Amy was bright and flirty and outgoing, and Willa was quiet and naïve and a lot less boisterous than her friend. She couldn't just spill all the beans about her less than happy marriage—not even with Amy, so successful, confident, sophisticated. With Amy those qualities went deeper than her looks and clothes right into her psyche. Unlike Willa, whose confidence and sophistication was just a fabric layer deep.

'I wanted to be something other than his pretty arm decoration. He didn't see why being that wasn't enough for me.'

'It got ugly. I called him a balding, ageing git and he called me a shallow bimbo. The words "separation" and "divorce" emerged and we were both very happy with the idea.'

Amy closed her eyes in sympathy. 'Sorry, Wills.'

Willa shrugged. 'Eight months ago he booted me out of our apartment and into a waterfront mansion in Vaucluse—'

Amy whistled at the mention of the very upmarket Sydney suburb. 'Why didn't *he* move into the waterfront property?'

Willa smiled. 'He hates water and open spaces. Anyway, he moved Young and Dumb into the apartment the afternoon I moved out. Now the divorce just needs its court date and I'll be free!'

'What are you going to do then?'

Willa shrugged. 'Still working that out… I have a degree, but no experience, and—worse—no contacts. Money is not a problem, but time is. I battle to fill my day, and rattling around on my own in that mausoleum doesn't help.'

She glanced at the Rolex on her wrist, a twenty-first birthday present from Wayne. It was boring enough living her life, she didn't need to dissect it as well, so she attempted to change the subject.

'We've been in here for about twenty minutes. Do you think my date from hell has got the hint?'

'I told Guido to tell him that you weren't interested.'

Amy shrugged at Willa's quick, questioning look.

'Hey, you wanted to make his brain explode. I thought I'd save you a prison sentence.'

'True,' Willa admitted as she stood up. 'Okay, well… it was great seeing you but I suppose I should get home.'

'To do more rattling?' Amy shook her head. 'Oh, hell, no. If I ever saw someone in need of a party it's you. I've just signed a huge PR deal—'

'You're in PR? You're far too self-effacing, modest and shy for PR, Ames,' Willa said, her voice deceptively gentle.

Amy just laughed, and instantly catapulted Willa back the best part of a decade. It was a killer laugh—dirty as mud.

'There's that sarcastic mouth I used to love. Anyway, I've just signed a huge deal to launch a new franchise of sports shops selling clothes and equipment—my client is also setting up some hardcore men-only gyms—and a couple of my workmates and I are going out to celebrate. We're taking my new client clubbing. And *you* are going to join us!'

'Uh, I don't think so…'

'I do! My client's name is Rob, he's gorgeous and gruff—but not my type, unfortunately.' Amy led her out of the pretty function room and back towards the main dining area. 'He might be yours.'

Willa scoffed. 'If he's like any of the men I've recently come into contact with he'll need a hug…around the neck… with a rope.'

'Am really *loving* this whole bloodthirsty serial killer vibe you've got going.' Amy shot her a grin. 'I sense sexual frustration.'

Willa grinned at her. 'I sense that I am going to kick you soon.'

Amy tucked her arm into Willa's as they walked towards the exit. 'Oh, yeah…the girls are back in town. And it seems like I am going to have to teach you how to party… to cut loose.'

'Again.'

Rob Hanson looked at the sharply dressed partygoers dutifully lining up outside Fox, waiting in anxious anticipation to get into the popular club, and shook his head. Pulling on a pair of Levi's and a button-down white shirt with its sleeves rolled up was about as dressed up as he got…besides, it wasn't what you looked like that got you into a club—unless you were female and had a great cleavage, blonde hair down to your waist and legs up to your neck— it was attitude…

And he had lots of it.

Rob caught the eye of a bouncer, jerked his head and received a quick nod to go in, bypassing the queue. He slipped a bill into the guy's hand in a slick movement as the rope was lifted and cursed when his mobile vibrated in his pocket. Stepping back from the door, he shoved his finger in his ear and answered the call.

'Rob, it's Gail.'

'Hey, Snail.' At twenty-two, his sister was ten years younger than him and the best thing in his life. 'What's up?'

'Not much—just checking in,' Gail replied. 'Whatcha doing?'

'About to go into a club.'

'Have you met anyone yet?' Gail demanded.

'I haven't even been here two days!' he protested.

'My man-about-town bachelor brother is slacking,' Gail teased and he rolled his eyes.

'I won't have the time in Sydney and I don't have the inclination,' Rob retorted.

Gail's laugh tickled his ear. 'Did the screaming match with Saskia put you off? Judging by the way she flounced out of here, she obviously didn't take it well when you told her that she'd hit her expiry date?'

'Jeez, Gail! Her *expiry date*?'

'I call it like I see it. You never go over the three-month-fling mark and she was due.'

Not as obsessed with the time-frames of his dates as his sister, Rob counted back. Yeah, it *was* nearly dead on three months. He'd started getting twitchy as Saskia started making noises about 'formalising' their relationship, dropping comments about needing cupboard space in his bedroom. She had left a box of tampons in his bathroom cabinet and he'd realised that it was time to bail. She wasn't someone he wanted around long-term…

He'd never met anyone he wanted around long-term.

'One day you're going to meet someone who blows your socks off,' Gail warned him.

He doubted it. Remembering that the best way to get Gail off the subject of his love-life was to comment on hers, he said: 'Are you still dating the tattoo artist? Does he make enough money to take you to the movies occasionally?'

Gail sighed. 'Well-played. Deflect and distract.'

'I try. Don't do anything stupid with this one, okay, honey?'

After witnessing the best and worst of love, he and

Gail approached relationships from opposite directions. She thought that true love and happily-ever-after was just around the corner, and he knew that there was only one person he could ever fully depend on and that was himself.

He and Gail adored each other, but they didn't understand the other's choices when it came to the opposite sex.

'How long are you going to be in Sydney?' Gail asked. 'This house is like a morgue without you.'

'A month…six weeks,' Rob replied. 'Do not let Mr Body Art move in while I'm gone.'

Gail laughed again. 'I'll just move into his place… Bye—love you!'

Rob looked at his dead phone and shook his head. He was convinced that Gail only called him to wind him up and raise his blood pressure. That, he supposed, was a younger sister's job.

Rob looked at his watch…ten p.m. here, and that meant it would be around two in the afternoon back home. Snail was home from her morning classes at uni and she was bored—and a great way to relieve that boredom was to take pot-shots at his love-life.

Revenge, Rob decided as he stepped into the heaving club, would be sweet and designed to embarrass her to the max. Because that was what his job as her older brother was.

Slapped in the face with the noise and smell of the club—alcohol and perfume and sweat mixed together in an almost palpable fug—he immediately asked himself what he was doing. Apart from the fact that he was still exhausted from the long flight from Johannesburg the day before yesterday—he really had to learn to sleep on planes—and the fact that he'd been working sixteen-hour days for months, he also hated clubs and clubbing.

Too loud, too packed, girls too obvious and generally far too young and too eager. Call him old-fashioned but he liked to do a little work before a piece of tail fell into his lap. And, really, at thirty-two, dating kids his sister's age or younger made him feel like a dirty old man.

Rob brushed off a hand on his behind and ignored a proposition from his left as he scanned the bar. He'd find his new firecracker of a PR person, make his excuses and then head back to the flat he'd rented and fall face-down onto the bed.

Rob ran a hand over his short dark brown curls and squinted into the low light of the club. Finding Amy in this madhouse was going to be a nightmare, he thought as his mobile vibrated in his pocket. Or not, he thought, looking at the text message.

At the entrance, hook a left and head towards the back of the club. Table in the back corner.

God bless technology. Rob smiled, shoved his mobile back into the pocket of his jeans and took her directions.

Ah, a table full of women…not too young, thank God, but obviously, judging by the bottles and glasses on the table, well on their way to being cabbaged. *Shoot me now,* he thought. Half an hour, one beer, and he was out of there.

At least they were gorgeous women, admittedly. Amy, confident and glossy, led the pack. There was her colleague—he couldn't remember her name—and her assistant. Couldn't remember her name either. The other two women he didn't recognise at all. He dismissed the tomboy blonde who, he saw when he looked over his shoulder, was swapping some major eye contact with some dude at the bar, and focussed on the woman with mahogany hair tucked into the corner of the table, a cocktail glass in her hand. She had a wide-eyed, Audrey Hepburn waif look to her that instantly made a man regress to being a caveman.

You woman, I protect you. Lie down and I make you happy. Grunt. Grunt.

He'd known a lot of women—sue him…he was in his thirties and had been consistently single all his life—so he was old enough and wise enough to realise that waifs and strays, romantics and women who seemed helpless and hopeless, normally ended up tearing strips off him.

Women, as he'd learnt, were seldom what they portrayed themselves to be. Scrap that. *People* mostly weren't who they said they were.

Amy sprang to her feet. 'Rob—yay, you're here!'
Yeah. Yay.

'You know Bella and Kara, my colleagues—' their names went in one ear and out of the other '—the creature ignoring you for the rock star wannabe at the bar is my flatmate Jessica—oi! Jessica! This is Rob.'

The blonde whipped her head around, flashed him a smile. 'Hey, Rob.'

Quick eye contact and a super-fast scan to determine whether she found him attractive. She hesitated, suggesting that she did, but then her eyes slid back to the bar. Rob smiled inwardly. Someone, if he played his cards right, was getting lucky tonight.

Amy touched his wrist to get his attention. 'And this is my old, old friend Willa. Willa, this is Rob Hanson.'

'You make me sound like a crone with all the olds, Ames,' Willa complained good-naturedly, before lifting amazing silver-shot-with-green eyes to his. 'Hi.'

'Hi back.'

Rob took the open seat next to her and eyed the full beer bottle on the table, icy cold. It was his favourite brand.

He cocked an eyebrow at Amy. 'That for me?'

'Sure.' Amy pushed the bottle and glass across the table. Ignoring the glass and picking up the bottle, he lifted it to his lips and allowed the liquid to slide down his throat. One beer, half an hour and he'd leave…

'Rob owns a chain of sports equipment and clothing stores in South Africa, Willa. And some gyms. He's looking for franchisees to open branches of the stores everywhere, and the gyms will be here in Sydney, Perth and Melbourne initially.'

'Brave…' Willa murmured. 'Especially the gym part, since the marketplace is dominated by Just Fit. And Just Fit has gone on an acquisition drive to buy up the rats and mice gyms that aren't allowing them marketplace domination.'

Rob lowered his bottle and sent her a long look. Then he lifted his eyebrows at Amy, who just laughed.

'She's not just a pretty face,' she said.

Intriguing…

And she wasn't done. 'It takes a set of brass balls to take on two competitors, firmly established and synonymous with Australian health and fitness, one of which is about to list on the ASX. I intend to buy some of their shares when they go public in…' Smarty-Pants squinted at her watch '…six weeks' time.'

Rob just stared at her as she rested her chin in the palm of her hand and gave Amy a puppy-dog look. '*I* want a set of brass balls, Ames. How do I acquire my own?'

Amy threw back her head and laughed. 'Wills, how many of those Screaming Orgasms have you had?'

Willa slid her eyes to the row of cocktail glasses in front of her and counted them off. 'Not enough real ones and four fake ones.'

Willa and Amy exchanged a long look before they both bellowed with laughter.

Oh, jeez—drunk girl humour. About orgasms. Shoot him now. But he had to admit it wasn't fake girl laughter but a real, joyous exchange of humour between two friends

who understood each other's subtext. Their laughter made
him smile.

'So how long have you been friends?' he asked, picking
at the corner of his beer label with a short, blunt fingernail.

He hoped that his question would distract them from
further Screaming Orgasm humour—especially since, A.
He hadn't had one recently, and B. He'd just decided to stay
for another beer, another half-hour.

'Eight, nearly nine years—with far too many lost years
in between,' Willa replied.

Seeing the confusion on his face, she placed her hand
on his bare forearm and—*whoa*! What the hell…? Lust and
attraction shot up his arm and exploded in his brain. He
went stock-still and tried to work through his reaction. He'd
never, since the time he'd found out that girls had fun things
he liked to play with, had such a rocketing blood from his
head reaction to the simple touch of fingers on his skin.

He looked at her again and realised that she wasn't just
pretty—she was damn sexy. High cheekbones, a pouty
mouth and those amazing siren eyes. He allowed his own
eyes the pleasure of skimming over smooth shoulders,
smallish breasts and that too thin but utterly feminine body.

He tipped his head slightly to the side and saw that her
sage-green sleeveless dress disappeared under the table. He
needed to see more. On the pretext of bending sideways to
scratch his foot, he looked under the table. The dress ended
mid-thigh and, holy Moses, those legs were long and toned.
Since one nude heel had dropped off a slim foot, he saw
that her toes were tipped in tropical orange polish.

Hot, *hot*.

'…and then Amy left the Whitsundays—'

Rob blinked as he lifted his head and came back to the
conversation. He was both amused and irritated with himself. He never went on mental walkabouts—and especially
not over women.

'You're going to have to back up, Wills. Rob didn't hear a damn thing,' Amy drawled, lifting her beer bottle to her lips and raising a knowing eyebrow in his direction.

Rob felt an urge to pull out his tongue at her, which he manfully suppressed. He quickly rewound and took a stab in the dark. 'So, have you kept in contact with your other mates from those days?'

'Well, I talk to Luke my brother all the time. He was the resort manager.'

Amy sat up straighter and leaned forward. Hmm, Rob thought, interesting reaction to the mention of his name. Something churning there.

'We barely talk nowadays, but I have all their e-mail addresses, and I'm friends with them on social media,' Willa answered, her lips around a purple straw.

Rob, forcing the mental picture of what he'd really like to see those lips wrapped around from his mind, thought that there was no way he could go so long without connecting with his own tight circle of friends.

'You all should get together some time—catch up.'

Amy clapped her hands together with delight. 'That's such a fantastic idea. We should do that, Wills. We can invite them for a barbie…it'll be a Whitsundays reunion,' Amy gushed.

'Let's do it! When?' Willa asked, eyes sparkling.

'The sooner the better… Tomorrow is Sunday! A perfect day for a barbie by the pool…beers, bikinis… We can have a seafood Barbie,' Amy babbled. 'Invite them, Willa! *Now!* I betcha they will all come.'

Willa reached for her bag, her enthusiasm elevated by those Screaming Orgasms. She pulled out the latest smartphone and Rob raised his eyes as her fingers flew over the touchscreen. 'Okay, I've tagged Scott and Brodie and Chantal. Luke is in Singapore, the jerk. Who else?'

'The bartenders—Matt and Phil. Invite them! They were

fun… Tell them to bring booze for cocktails.' Amy leaned forward. 'And Jane and Gwen who were part of the entertainment crew.' Amy looked at Rob. 'We were quite sure that they provided extra "entertainment" to the guests, but they were such a riot.'

'And the lifeguards—I hope they're still hot! Tagged them… Come on, Ames, there were at least twenty of us who ran wild… I've tagged the girls who helped me entertain the rug rats.'

'The rug rats?' Rob asked.

'I looked after the kids at the resort… I kept them entertained so that their parents could have a break. And afternoon sex,' Willa explained without looking up from her smartphone. 'Come on, Amy—think!'

Amy rattled off a few more names and Willa bobbed her head in excitement. 'Okay, anyone else?'

'Nah. I think that's it.'

Amy leaned back in her chair and looked over to her flatmate. She let out a loud whistle that felt like an ice pick in Rob's brain, but it had the desired effect and Jessica turned around.

'Hey, Jess, want to go to a barbie with me and Willa?'

'Sure,' Jessica replied, turning to Willa. 'When?'

'Tomorrow. What time?' Willa asked Amy.

'Eleven. Bring your own bottle,' Amy replied, and Rob watched, amused, as their impromptu party started to take shape.

Whether their guests would appreciate—or accept—an invitation at half-ten at night for a party the next day was another story, but it was fun watching their cocktail-induced excitement. That being said, he knew that they were *so* going to regret their impulsiveness in the morning, when their heads woke them up, screaming that they had had brain surgery without anaesthetic.

'Okay, eleven...bring my own bottle...where?' Jessica asked.

'Yeah, where? Maybe I should add that.' Willa squinted at her phone.

'That would be helpful,' Rob murmured, but no one heard him.

Amy pretended to think, her eyes dancing. 'Oh, I don't know...who do we know who has an empty Sydney waterfront property with a pool?'

Willa shrugged. 'Who?'

Then the penny dropped with a clang and Willa bounced up and down in her chair like a first-grader.

'Oooh, *I* do! Me! Me, me, me, me...*me*!'

'Attagirl.' Amy lifted her bottle in her direction.

Even Rob, stranger that he was to the city, knew that waterfront property in Sydney meant big bucks. Who *was* this waif? An heiress? A celebrity?

'Hey, if I'm finally going to host a party of my own then I'm going to invite who I want to invite,' Willa stated emphatically. 'Like Kate!'

'Who's Kate?' Amy asked.

Yeah, who is Kate, gorgeous?

'My lawyer.'

Why would a woman in her mid to late twenties have her own lawyer? Interesting... Then again, the whole package was fascinating... Brains and beauty and those brilliant legs that were made to wrap around a man's hips...

Okay, slow down there, Hanson.

Willa's phone beeped and her face fell. 'Poop. Kate can't come. Oh, well.' She looked around for a waiter. 'I need another drink.'

Some liver pills, a litre of water and a few painkillers wouldn't hurt either, Rob told her silently.

CHAPTER TWO

SHE WASN'T DRUNK, Willa told herself. Happy, relaxed… slightly buzzed, maybe, but not drunk. And she was having fun, she realised on a happy sigh. *Fun*… She rolled the word around her tongue. Well…hello, there, stranger.

She was twenty-six years old—jeez, nearly twenty-seven—and she'd played the part of young, gorgeous, thick trophy wife all her adult life because Wayne and what he'd wanted had been important…her, not so much.

She was a great example of why you shouldn't be in charge of your own destiny when you were too young and too dumb to be making decisions more complicated than how to operate a teaspoon.

Willa pushed her heavy hair back from her face. She'd stopped loving Wayne years and years ago, and now she just wished she could finally be free of him—legally, mentally, comprehensively. And when she was she could fully enjoy men like…Rob.

Willa sneaked a look at that face and swallowed her lusty sigh. He was scruffy in all the right places, she thought. Sable-coloured curls that she longed to touch to see if they felt as soft as they looked, a four-day-old beard, a shirt that skimmed long muscles and tanned skin, giving hints of well-defined pecs, and an impressive six-pack.

Those grey piercing eyes seemed to be shockingly observant and yet basically unreadable.

Rough, rugged, and completely at ease in his skin. She couldn't help but to compare him to the only other man she'd ever slept with—she was biggest of big girl's blouses!—and it was like comparing instant coffee to Mountain Blue. Simply an exercise in stupidity.

Wayne was smart Italian suits and hair gel to cover the bald patch on the crown of his head. Cologne, cufflinks and designer labels. Rob was...*not*. He didn't need to accessorise—he was excellent just as he was.

Sexy. Masculine. Nuclear-hot.

'Honey, you keep looking at me like that and I'm going to have to do something about it.'

Willa blinked as his drawling voice pulled her back into the moment and she noticed Amy leaving the table with a tall blond guy. They were heading towards the dance floor in the centre of the club. When had that happened? Maybe while she'd been spending the last five minutes drooling over Nuclear-Hot across the table.

She turned back to Rob and blinked like an owl. 'Hi...' she whispered.

'Hi back. You okay?'

'Mmm. I'm having fun. I haven't had fun for a long, long time.' Willa tapped her fingers on the table in time to the music. 'Do you dance?'

Rob's mobile mouth kicked up. 'If I have to.'

Willa looked from the dance floor to him and nibbled on the bottom of her lip. The last time she'd danced—really danced, with feeling and heart and soul—had been in the Whitsundays at that dive bar where all the staff employed at the hotels in the area had congregated to hook up, break up, kiss and make up.

She wanted to feel young again—eighteen again—when the nights had been long and had held a myriad of possibilities.

She wanted to dance with Rob...

Maybe it was the cocktails making her feel brave. If it was she'd have another three or four Screaming Os, thank you very much. *Then you'd be face-down on the floor*, commented doormat Willa.

Willa took a breath and blurted out her question. 'Will you dance…with me?'

Rob immediately rose to his feet and held out his hand.

Willa took a moment to find her shoe before standing up and placing her hand in his much bigger one. She followed in his wake as he pushed through the packed crowds to the edge of the dance floor. Instead of finding a spot on the edge, Rob pulled her into the centre of the floor, flashed her a grin and started to move.

Willa stared at him in shock as he immediately picked up the beat and moved his hips in a sinuous rhythm that dried up all the moisture in her mouth. Dear Lord, those hips… If he took the same skill to the bedroom he would be declared a lethal sexual weapon in several countries.

'I thought you said you don't dance!' Willa shouted.

Rob flashed her a smile as his shoulders lifted and rolled. 'I said that I dance if I have to.'

Willa stepped closer to him so that she could speak directly in his ear. 'You're pretty good.'

'Just one of my talents.'

Rob placed his hands on her hips and before she knew it her thigh was between his and they were rocking together. Willa swallowed the lump in her throat as Rob's hand lifted to encircle her neck, using his thumb to push her jaw up so that their eyes met. Willa wasn't that out of practice that she couldn't recognise the attraction in his eyes, the accelerated pulse under the wrists she loosely held.

'Man…you are seriously gorgeous. And to think that I nearly blew this off,' Rob muttered, mostly to himself, as his other hand slid around her back and yanked her towards him so that their bodies were pressed flush against each other.

His chest was wider and bigger and harder than hers,

Willa thought as she dropped her nose to the V of skin his shirt revealed and inhaled his man smell, his heat. Lust boiled and roiled and her happy place throbbed, echoing the beat of the music. His surprisingly soft chest hair tickled her nose and she felt rather than heard the rumble of a moan in his chest, his throat. One hand splayed across her back, between her shoulder blades, and the other dropped lower onto her ass, holding her firmly in place against him. And that, she could feel, made him *very* happy indeed.

Somehow he kept them swaying to the beat, pretending to dance.

'So, twenty questions time?'

Rob's deep voice in her ear did nothing to assuage the heat between her legs—in fact it sped up her sluggish blood.

Questions? Was he mad? Between him and the cocktails she'd didn't have an operational brain cell left.

'Yes...no...I don't know,' Willa murmured back.

'Wrong, wrong and wrong,' Rob responded with an appreciative grin. 'Let's try that again. Why do you have a lawyer?'

She didn't feel like explaining about Wayne and her imminent divorce. She wasn't going to see Rob again after tonight, but she still thought it would be tacky to explain about her ex while she was pressed up very close and very personal against him. Besides, she didn't want memories of Wayne to taint this experience of her first fun night out in for ever. Her ex and her old life were in the past.

Rob was here—now.

Carpe diem, Willa.

'Pass.'

'Okay...next one. What do you do that you're such an expert on the health and fitness market? Stockbroker? Financial analyst?'

She wished—she really, *really* wished.

'I read. A lot.' Even she, novice that she was at this flirting and seduction stuff, knew that he didn't need to know that reading finance and business magazines was one of her favourite ways to pass some time. Willa squinted at him and pulled a face. 'These are very boring questions…'

Rob laughed. 'Okay, then—you hit me with one.'

Willa sucked in her cheeks. There were a million things she wanted to know about him, but the least important flew out of her mouth.

'Boxers or briefs?'

Bad girl, Willa.

Rob's laugh brushed over her skin.

'Why don't you drop your hands and find out?' Rob suggested, and her face immediately pinked up. Taking one of her hands from his neck, he guided it around his hips and slapped it on his butt. 'Feel free to explore.'

Oh, that was a mighty fine ass, she thought as she took him up on his offer. Hard, muscular…male.

'What do you sleep in?' he asked, his breath teasing her ear.

A pair of sleep shorts and a ratty T-shirt. That wasn't sexy, Willa thought. She tossed back her hair and widened her eyes as she prepared to lie. 'I sleep naked. All… the…time.'

His eyes dilated and Willa remembered how much fun it was to flirt, to tease, how thrilling it was to get a hard-eyed and hard man—in every way that counted—all flustered. Sometimes being a girl was such a kick.

'Bet you look damn good naked.'

'I do. As, I suspect…' Willa gave his butt a squeeze '…do you.'

In her head wild Willa tried to high-five doormat Willa, but she was banging her head against an imaginary wall.

Rob let out a muffled groan and rested his forehead on hers. 'How hot is it, exactly, in here?'

'It's cookin',' Willa agreed, surprised at their effortless banter, her ability to flirt so easily.

Maybe it was the Screaming Os, the obvious appreciation and attraction in Rob's eyes, his hot hands sliding over her arms, back, hips, that made her feel bolder and brighter—the best version of herself. Confident, slightly crazy, prepared to take a risk.

One night, she told herself. Didn't she deserve one night of uncomplicated pleasure with a hot man who looked as if he wanted to gobble her up in one big bite? *Hell, yes!* shouted wild Willa, thoroughly over-excited. Didn't she deserve a night of stupendous sex after more than eight months of sexual drought? Her house was empty, her bed was empty...she was all but free.

You betcha, sister!

Doormat Willa groaned and slapped her hand over her eyes.

Before she could lose her courage and change her mind, Willa tipped her head back and nailed him with her silver-green eyes. 'Got condoms?'

'Yes. Why?' Rob replied carefully as his hands tightened on her hips. 'You offering to let me use a couple?'

'Yeah...you interested?'

Rob sucked in a breath. 'Yeah—to the max. I've been thinking about it...'

'Since when?'

'I've been having X-rated fantasies about your fabulous legs encircling my hips since I first clocked them.' He stepped back and looked at her legs. When he lifted his eyes again they'd turned sombre and serious. 'You sure about this, Willa? Why do I have the feeling that this isn't the way you normally operate?'

It isn't—we don't know what we're doing here! Doormat Willa wrung her hands, whimpering.

Well, she wasn't in charge tonight. Wild Willa was going to have some fun. 'I'm very sure.'

Relief flashed across Rob's face. 'Where would you feel more comfortable? My place or yours?'

Oh, her place—absolutely. And if she was silently raising her middle finger to her ex by sleeping with someone else in a bed that he'd paid for, then nobody had to know but her.

Oh, dear God, she was *sleeping with someone else…* someone other than her forty-something husband who didn't exactly encourage creativity in bed. Mr Missionary Position, she'd privately called him. Wham, bam…skip the thank-you, ma'am.

Rob's thumb brushing her cheekbone pulled her back to reality. 'Hey, where did you go?'

Willa grabbed his wrist. It was only fair to give him a heads-up so that he didn't feel cheated when he realised that she was more below par than porn star. 'Look, you should know that I don't do this…often.' *Try never.* 'And I'm not…'

'Not what?'

'Experienced.'

Rob looked at her for a long time without saying anything. Before he spoke, he brushed her lips with a kiss and Willa quivered. 'Feel that?' he murmured against her mouth. 'Feel the electricity between us?'

'Mmm-hmm.'

'I'm old enough and experienced enough to know that doesn't happen often, and when it does you don't need anything else but to give yourself over to it. But, since you were honest enough to tell me that you aren't a pro at this, let me remind you of the rules.'

There are rules? God! Seriously? Her lower lip pushed out. Wild Willa didn't like rules.

'Okay,' Willa agreed, although she'd really much prefer Rob just to kiss her again.

'This is a one-night thing, so no thinking about hearts and flowers.'

Willa felt the power of his honest statement.

'I'm attracted to you, and the little I've seen of you, I like. I don't sleep with women I don't like, but tonight is it…there will be nothing more than a couple of laughs and some good sex.'

'*Good* sex is the minimum I require,' Willa said, making herself sound innocent.

Rob's lips twitched. 'Why do I suspect that when you widen those eyes and sound naïve you are at your most sarcastic?'

Because he wasn't a fool, Willa realised, but she didn't confirm or deny his statement.

'And if you change your mind at any point—any point at all!—you say so and I back off. I can't guarantee that I'll be happy about it, but I'll back off. You don't like anything I do, you say so and I don't do it again.'

Willa blinked. 'My God, you are direct.'

'No point in being anything else,' Rob retorted. 'I'm uncomfortably honest, or so I've frequently been told. It's the only way I know how to be. Can you handle that?'

After the last eight years, honesty was a brilliant change of pace. 'Since you're only going to be around for the rest of the night, I think I can cope.'

Rob grinned at her jibe. 'There's that gentle sarcasm again…I love it. So, let's go—so that I can get you naked sooner rather than later.'

Willa felt his hand wrap around hers—solid, masculine and sure—and she allowed him to tug her off the dance floor and towards the exit of the club.

We're gonna get laid, Wild Willa shouted, *thoroughly thrilled. Whooo-hooo!*

Willa didn't bother to switch on any lights as she entered the double-volume hallway of her Vaucluse waterfront property—she just kicked the door closed behind Rob and immediately reached for him.

They'd found a taxi as they'd left the club and a heated silence had filled the interior of the vehicle. Yet she hadn't needed words to know that he couldn't wait to get his hands on her. His warm hand had started off on her bare knee and slowly worked its way up her thigh, so that when the taxi had pulled up in front of the massive mansion her dress had been skimming her crotch line and his fingers had been not too far from her happy place.

Now she was damp and hot and horny, and if she didn't get him touching her soon she was going to cry like a little girl.

Rob, finding her plastered against his chest, didn't need any encouragement and immediately yanked her dress up and palmed her butt with his masterful hand. He shoved his other hand into her heavy mass of hair, clasped her head and angled her face to receive his no-holds-barred kiss. Tongues danced as he devoured her mouth, learning her, tasting her, pushing her for more.

Emboldened by his passion and his groans of appreciation, Willa pulled his shirt up so that she could touch his hot body. So hard, she thought. Muscular, but not over the top…just pure masculine strength. Her fingers traced the rows of his six-pack and the long muscles that covered his hips, brushed over the hard erection that tented his jeans.

Ooh, she liked that, so she traced his long length with the tip of her finger. Yeah, she liked that. *A lot.*

'Yeah, that's it,' Rob muttered against her mouth, pulling her dress up and over her hips, revealing her tiny black thong to his hungry gaze.

His hands gripped and released her hips as he looked down at her, past her flat stomach to her long legs. She was still in her heels.

'Perfect,' he breathed. 'Is the rest of you as pretty, Willa?'

'Maybe,' Willa replied, undoing his belt buckle.

Rob slid his hand between her legs and cupped her, his thumb immediately finding and brushing her clitoris through her thong, causing her to yelp into her mouth.

'So good...so good,' Willa moaned against his lips. 'More...more.'

Rob's hand stilled and his breath was hot and laboured. 'If we don't stop now I'm going to yank these off and take you right here, right now. Against the front door or on this Persian carpet under our feet.'

Willa tipped her head back to look up into his fabulous passion-soaked steel-coloured eyes. 'Yeah...either. Both. Just do it *now*.'

Rob smiled and reached for the foil strip of condoms he'd shoved into the back pocket of his jeans. He ripped a packet off with his teeth and allowed the rest to drop to the floor. He placed it in her hand with a wicked grin.

'Put it on me while I get rid of your panties.'

Willa popped open the first button of his jeans, then the second, and when they were loose around his hips she shoved her hands inside his briefs and pushed both his underwear and jeans down. His erection stood tall and proud, and Willa sighed at how big he was... It seemed that Wayne wasn't nearly as well-endowed as he'd claimed. Well, he'd lied about everything else so she wasn't particularly surprised.

But Rob was long and thick, and she knew that taking him inside her meant she would have to stretch and... She licked her lips... She couldn't wait. She wanted to be pushed, filled, taken to the limit. She wanted to feel like a woman being possessed by a man...in the best way possible.

Willa ripped the packet open with her teeth, pulled out the condom and swiftly rolled it over his penis, sucking in her breath as he hardened even further.

Above her head, Rob swore. 'Honey, this is going to be hectic…we'll keep slow and sexy for later.'

With those words, he hooked his big hands under her thighs and lifted her up, spreading her legs so that the head of his penis probed her wet and moist feminine core. It was only then that Willa realised he'd magicked her panties away without her even realising…

Rob pressed her against the massive wooden front door and pinned her there with his body, sliding into her with one long, sure stroke. Willa felt herself dissolving from the inside out as her world narrowed to what was happening between them. Her surroundings faded away and there were only Rob's hands on her thighs, his tongue in her mouth mimicking his thrust of his hips, the sure strokes as he lifted her higher and higher.

'You need to come, honey, 'cos I'm not going to be able to hang on,' Rob muttered, his forehead against hers.

'Don't you dare stop!' Willa shot back, grinding down on him as lightning bugs danced along her skin.

Rob dropped his head to talk in her ear. 'That's it, Willa, take all of me. Yeah, move…use me…higher, dammit!'

'Harder…' Willa demanded, reaching for her release.

Rob slammed her against the door and she shouted as stars exploded behind her eyeballs and her body splintered into a million billion pieces. She vaguely heard Rob's roar in her ear, felt his orgasm deep inside her, but didn't particularly care. She'd come and it had been magnificent…

Rob moved his hips again and, still mostly hard, touched something inside her. She rocketed up again, harder and faster than before. She slammed her eyes shut and screamed his name before she fractured again in a big bang of cosmic proportions.

Minutes, hours or years might have passed before she came back down to earth, her head on his shoulder, pinned to the door by Rob's strength.

'I really don't think you hit the mark, Willa. We might have to do that again.'

She heard Rob's smile in his words, felt the curve of his lips against her temple.

'Slow and sexy this time?' Willa agreed on a happy smile, sliding to the floor.

Early the next morning, after another round of blow-her-head-off morning sex, Willa, her head on Rob's shoulder, felt well satisfied with herself. She thought that she'd feel dirty and guilty, going to bed with a complete stranger, but all she felt was...satisfied—and strangely safe.

Sure, he was good-looking—what was the point of having a one-night stand with an ugly man?—and he had a body that spoke of a lifetime of physical fitness. He smelt good, and he had treated her with care and made sure that that she was fully satisfied—every single time—before climaxing himself.

He was as close to a perfect lover as she'd ever encountered—okay, *that* didn't mean anything at all!—and she idly wondered whether it was his skill in the sack or her previous lack of satisfactory sex that had had her coming over and over again.

She suspected that it was mostly Rob. He was an amazing lover. She'd felt safe enough to allow herself to lose control—to touch, to explore, to taste—and she had lost all her inhibitions in her quest to explore those long, lean muscles. That had never happened to her before.

With Wayne... *No.* No comparisons—no thinking about him.

Suffice to say that with Rob she felt energised. Sleep had been forgotten in the delight of his body. She remembered thinking that she hadn't wanted the feast of touch and textures and taste and masculinity to end.

She still didn't.

'I need sustenance,' Willa said on a long yawn. 'What's the time?'

'Half-eight.'

Rob patted her butt to get her to move. He slid out of bed and walked across the ridiculously enormous bedroom to the balcony doors. He gripped the top of the doorframe and Willa rolled over on her stomach to look at his beautiful back, tight ass and long, muscular legs.

Hot damn, the man was sexy. Willa licked her lips and was suddenly conscious of her pounding head and the fact that her mouth felt as if a herd of llamas had bedded down in it during the night.

'This is a hell of place you have here, Willa. Yours?'

'Yeah.' Well, it would be in a few weeks' time.

This massive house she'd moved into eight months ago still didn't feel like her home. But the exclusive property would form part of her divorce settlement—along with her Mercedes and a hefty donation to her bank account. She'd wanted to walk away with nothing, just to get rid of Wayne, but Kate, her lawyer and now a good friend, had refused to allow her even to go there.

'He cheats, he pays,' Kate had told her, over and over again.

'Where exactly are we?' Rob asked. 'Is that Sydney harbour bridge?'

'Yep.'

Willa stood up, wrapped a sheet around her torso and ducked under his arm to move onto the veranda off the bedroom.

She leaned against the railing and pointed down to the jetty that kissed the crystal-clear water below. 'At the end of the garden is a gate that leads onto that path, and via that jetty I have direct access to Parsley Bay. I can swim, snorkel, kayak, or picnic in the beautiful neighbouring parkland.'

Willa turned her back to the bay and looked at him.

'It's a big house on a big plot of land—six bedrooms, four bathrooms, lots of living space and decks. Double garage. Private.'

'And you live here all alone?' Rob asked, sceptical.

'Ridiculous, isn't it?' Willa replied lightly, not wanting to go into details about her failed marriage. 'The house is cold and empty and it should have kids running around in it, pets, people visiting and loud parties…'

'Well, it will today.'

Willa looked at him blankly.

Rob grinned and she caught a flash of white teeth and the glint of the sun in his stubble. 'Honey, you have a bunch of people arriving for a barbecue…' he looked at his watch '…later this morning.'

It took a moment for her to remember that she'd invited the entire Whitsundays gang—not just her old friends—for a barbecue this morning.

Grabbing Rob's wrist, she looked at the dial of his watch and let out a low wail of panic. She had nothing in her house to eat, no booze, and the fact that she had to entertain people she hadn't seen in years—not to mention dealing with this very sexy souvenir from the night below—had panic crawling up her throat.

She couldn't do this,—she really couldn't. Maybe she could hustle Rob out through the front door and she could escape out the back—hightail it to her canoe and belt her way up the bay.

Opening her mouth like a fish desperate for oxygen, she stared at Rob in horror.

'Take a breath, Willa,' Rob suggested on a slow grin.

Willa slapped her hands against her cheeks and gasped as the sheet dropped and fell over the lounger. Rob's eyes darkened with passion and his penis started to swell. Willa saw what was happening, lifted her hand and tried to step away from him—she really did. But her legs weren't doing much listening. In fact they were taking her to him!

'No! No! No, no, no, no, no, *no*! I don't have time, Rob!'

Rob's thumb drifted over her nipple and Willa felt her resolve weaken. How could she just look at him and feel prickly and horny and…wet? *Get a grip, Willa.* But one more time her body whispered its demand. One more thrilling, amazing orgasm or…four.

'I want to take you here, on this lounger, in the morning sun.'

'God, Rob… It's out in the open. The neighbours….'

Why was she even thinking about doing this? Was she mad?

'Nobody can see us, Willa. This balcony was built for privacy,' Rob said, sliding his hand between her thighs.

Willa instantly melted.

'Here…in the sun, Wills. Say yes.'

'Yes.' Willa sighed, looping her hands around his neck and slapping her naked body against his. As if she'd ever had any chance of saying no.

Ding-dong! Ding-dong!

Willa's eyes shot open and she bolted upright in bed. Fudge, was that the doorbell? That couldn't be the doorbell, there was no way that it was eleven already…

Ding-dong. Ding-dong.

Dammit, it *was* the doorbell, and the doorbell meant guests. *Arrrggghhhhh.* She was in such trouble…

Rob groaned and opened one eye. Willa glared down at him. 'This is your fault!' she hissed.

'Huh? Why?'

Willa shot out of bed and ran to her walk-in closet, reaching for clean underwear and a pair of shorts. Grabbing a denim pair that were more holes than fabric, she yanked them on.

'"I want to take you here, on this lounger, in the morning sun…"' Willa growled, imitating his deep voice. '"Just come back to bed for a little while," you said. "we have time," you said!'

'We must have dozed off.' Rob rolled over, taking the sheets with him, and squinted at his watch. 'Huh—ten-forty. Someone is early. Either way, it seems we're out of time.'

'You *think*, Einstein?' Willa barked, yanking on a tank top and pulling her hair up into a haphazard tail. 'I need a shower, to brush my teeth…'

'Slow down, gorgeous…' Rob suggested, standing up and stretching.

Willa glared at him as the doorbell chimed again. 'Keep your pants on,' she muttered, and then pointed to Rob. 'You too, hotshot.'

Rob grinned at her. 'I'm going to have a shower first…'

'I hate you!' Willa barked, before rushing out of the bedroom and down the stairs.

Through the stained glass windows of the door she could see two people on the other side. Yanking it open, she was relieved to see Amy and Jessica on her front steps.

'Thank God it's you!' she stated, holding her hand to her head, hoping to keep it from exploding. God, she had the headache from hell. What had been in those cocktails? Liquid mercury?

'Are you okay, Wills? You look…frazzled,' Amy said.

'I *am* frazzled,' Willa admitted. 'God, can I cancel this?'

Amy stepped into the double volume hall and whistled her appreciation as she turned in a circle. 'Hell, no, you're not cancelling a damn thing—and…wow, Wills, this house is a hell of a divorce settlement.'

'Kate's a hell of a divorce lawyer.'

And she wasn't letting Willa settle for just a house. She was, as she frequently told Willa, better and meaner than that.

Willa took a seat on the bottom step of the floating staircase. 'She's the sharpest tool in the shed; you'd like her, Amy.'

'If she's helping you bury Wayne-the-Pain then I like her already,' Amy agreed.

The Pain. *Such* an apt moniker.

'Anyway…can we concentrate, here? I have a cracking headache from those cocktails, I have God knows how many people arriving at any minute, and I have nothing— repeat, *nothing*!—in this house to feed or lubricate them.'

Amy frowned. 'Did you forget you invited us?'

'Sorta…kinda….yeah.' She couldn't tell her friend that she'd been having too much fun playing with Rob to think about her guests. 'What am I going to *dooooooo*?'

'You are going to go and have a shower. Jessica will greet anyone who arrives and Amy will shoot to the shops and grab food and drink.'

The deep, masculine, made-for-sin voice floated down the stairs.

Willa watched as Jessica and Amy's heads shot up and quickly turned to see Rob, his hair wet from his ultra-quick shower, dressed in his clothes from the night before, walking down the stairs, bare feet sticking out from the ragged hem of his jeans. Their surprise turned to feminine approval and she groaned as two sets of perfectly arched eyebrows lifted in a silent question.

'Way to go, Wills.'

Willa threw her hands up in defeat at Amy's mischievous murmur. 'Ah…Rob. Rob stayed over…'

'I can see that,' Amy stated with a grin.

Willa caught Amy's eye and saw the glint of sisterly pride in her eye. *So, didja have fun?* she could imagine her asking, if Jessica and Rob hadn't been there.

So much fun.

Thought you would. He looks the type who knows what he's doing.

You have no idea, old friend.

'You two done with your telepathic conversation?' Jessica demanded as she put out her hand and hauled Willa to her feet. 'Go shower, Willa. Amy, let's take a look and see what Willa has so that you know what to buy.'

'Nothing,' Willa said mournfully. 'I have nothing.'

'Why do *I* have to get the food?' Amy wailed.

'Because it was your idea to do this,' Willa retorted, hand still on her head. 'There's a deli down the road. They have everything... Just buy them out and I'll pay you back.'

Willa looked at Jessica and pointed to her left.

'Kitchen that way. Through the French doors of the kitchen—and off all the rooms on that side of the house—is a covered patio and the pool. Chairs, tables—all outside. Outside kitchen...grill. Go wild.'

Amy whistled her appreciation. 'As I said, Wills, it's a helluva settlement.'

Yeah, Willa thought as she climbed the stairs to the second floor and her bedroom. *All I had to do was put up with crap and be an aimless, thick trophy wife for eight years.*

CHAPTER THREE

ROB TOOK A call on his mobile and thought that if he didn't get coffee into his system in the next few minutes he'd find himself face-down on Willa's expensive floor, whimpering like a little girl.

He'd thought he had stamina—he regularly took part in triathlons, ran eight miles five days out of seven, and hit the gym several times a week. Yet rolling around in the sheets with Willa had sucked every last atom of energy from him...

Rob grinned. Best fun he'd had—in or out of bed—for ages.

But now coffee...*stat*. He'd grab a cup, kiss Willa goodbye and move on out. It was what he did and he did it well... He should—he'd had a hell of lot of practice at it.

Shoving his mobile into the back pocket of his jeans, he walked across the hall towards the feminine voices drifting down the passage from what he presumed was the kitchen.

'So, did you ever meet Willa's husband?'

Rob slammed to a stop and cursed... She was *married*? Crap, crap, crap. He didn't do married women—it was one of his *hell, no!* rules. She didn't wear a ring but...*crap*!

'About to be ex-husband,' Amy corrected, and he resumed breathing again. 'They've been separated for about eight months.'

Good—that was good. Not perfect, but a helluva lot better than married.

'What's he like?'

Rob leaned his shoulder into the wall a couple of me-

tres away from the kitchen door, knowing that if he went in
Willa's friends would stop talking. Girls tended not to dish
the dirt on about-to-be-exes when the guy one of them had
had a one-night stand with was in the room.

But he was curious.

He wanted more information on Willa, who interested
him far more than she should for a one-night stand. That
was something he needed to think about…but only when
he'd had coffee and a solid eight hours' sleep.

'Wayne… Yeah, I was with Willa when they met for
the first time.' Amy's voice had a faraway quality that suggested she was recalling memories from long ago.

'And?' Jessica's voice sounded impatient.

Amy took a while to answer and Rob mentally urged
her to get a move on.

'Slick,' Amy said eventually. 'Slick as snot. A lot older
than Willa—I think he was in his mid-thirties when they
first met…'

'You didn't like him,' Jessica stated.

'Yeah, instinctively didn't like him,' Amy agreed. 'I was
just frustrated, I guess. Willa was a kid so desperately in
need of fun, a good time, letting her hair down, and I was
showing her how to do that… God, we were having a blast!
Partying up a storm, flirting up a bigger storm…we ruled
the resort.'

'You mean *you* ruled and Willa was your sidekick,' Jessica said, dryly.

Rob grinned at that.

'Then she met Wayne and she… How do I explain
this? She shrank in on herself and became the perfect girlfriend—cool, calm, collected. With him she was eighteen
going on eighty. Crazy Willa left the building.'

'Since she was slamming down those cocktails last
night, I think crazy Willa is back,' Jessica said, and Rob
could hear the grin in her voice.

'Not by a long shot. And she wasn't anywhere near being drunk, trust me, that girl can hold her booze. When she's really drunk she ends up singing eighties ballads and taking her clothes off.'

Rob's eyebrows lifted with surprise. He'd like to see *that*.

'She can be a wild woman,' Amy added.

Rob had the nail-marks on his butt to prove *that* point.

'But with Wayne she stopped having fun. I suspect that last night was the first time she's had some real fun—proper fun—since she got married. She's a little sad, scared, and a lot lonely. I feel sort of protective of her...'

So did he.

Huh?

Rob looked down at his bare feet and instead of heading for the kitchen—caffeine, shockingly, could now wait—he walked through the sun room and headed for the sunlight-dappled deck: expensive outdoor furniture, a pizza oven built into the wall and an island holding a gas stove and a fridge. A ten-seater wooden dining table with benches on either side dominated the kitchen end of the deck, and cane couches and chairs with blue and white striped cushions filled the rest of the space. The large, rectangular pool looked cool and inviting and he wished he could dive into its clear depths.

He loved to swim—did some of his best thinking in the water.

So Willa had been married...was still, technically, married...to a guy who was a lot older than her and obviously rich. Her eyes held shadows within them that suggested long-term unhappiness; he recognised those shadows—he'd seen them in his mum's eyes every day she'd been married to Stefan.

Which was all on him. Because when she'd told him that Stefan had proposed, wondering what he thought, he'd said that she should take the plunge. Stefan had been his dad's best friend—*her* friend. Their second dad. She'd liked him, they'd liked him…what could go wrong? He'd just wanted her to be happy again, and—he had to be honest here—he'd known he would feel a lot more comfortable going off to uni across the country if he knew that Stefan was looking after Mum and Gail.

That hadn't worked out the way he'd thought it would.

When he'd finally got to the root of the problem—when his family had disintegrated around him for the second time—he'd felt his heart rip apart. It had been like losing his father all over again, and along with that he'd waved goodbye to his innocence and his faith in people.

And he'd kicked trust over a cliff.

Rob ran his hand along his scruffy jaw. Where was this coming from? He'd been thinking about Willa's sad eyes and then he'd started thinking of his past and his failure in the interpersonal relationships department.

Huh…

But the fact remained that he didn't like the idea of Willa feeling sad…

He'd slept with her once and he was already giving her more thought than he'd given all his past flings put together. Something was *very* wrong with this picture…

Because he didn't play games with other people—and especially with himself. He had to admit that he kind of liked the fact that Willa was still married, if only legally. It was a minor barrier, but a barrier nonetheless—something to help him keep his emotional distance, to remind him not to become any more involved than he should be. Than he liked to be, wanted to be, could afford to be…

One friggin' night and she's turning your head upside down. Get a grip, Hanson! You just want to sleep with her again, his sensible side argued. *There's no need to go all dark and broody and—what was the word Gail had used the other day?—'emo' about this. It's just sex. You know that after a couple of days you'll get bored and want to move on. So ask for another night, or two, or three, but just stop bloody brooding already. And get it into your thick block that she's no different from the others...*

Except that she is, he thought.

Very different... She *had* to be if he was thinking about her like this.

Rob dropped his long frame into the nearest chair and groaned loudly.

Get the hell out of her house and her life, moron, he told himself. *Now. You're looking for trouble—inviting complications in through the door. The night is over, the sun is high in the sky and if you're thinking that she is remotely special then your ass should be on fire, trying to get the hell away. Be smart about her, dude. Get your cup of coffee, say your goodbyes, and get the hell out of Dodge. You never stay this long—you rarely spend the night.*

Yet despite running through his long list of why he shouldn't be contemplating another night, a fling, a short-term affair with her, he was unable to walk away.

Rob placed his head on the back on the chair and groaned again. *You are utterly and completely screwed, man.*

Even that thought wasn't enough to pull himself out of the chair and out of her house.

Screwed to the max. And still caffeine-deprived.

Rob tapped on the frame of the open bathroom door and grinned when Willa, standing in front of the huge bathroom mirror above the double basins in a pale yellow bra and thong, reached for a dressing gown to cover up.

'Bit late for that, seeing as I've seen and kissed most of you.'

Fighting her blush, Willa dropped the gown. He had seen—stroked, tasted—everything, so it was a silly, pointless gesture. Willa picked up a square black box and, flipping it open, brushed a pale pink blush over her cheekbones. Rob placed a cup of coffee on the counter and went back to lean his shoulder into the doorframe and cross his legs at the ankles, holding his cup in his hand.

'Thanks,' Willa said.

'That was the last of the milk, and there's nothing but a half-tub of cottage cheese and some yoghurt in your fridge…what do you eat?'

'Not much,' she admitted in a jerky voice. 'I hate cooking for myself.'

Rob saw the confusion in her eyes, knew that she wasn't quite sure what to do with him, how to behave. While he knew her body inside out, he was still, to all intents and purposes, a stranger.

'So, some of your friends have arrived. Do you want me to go?'

Willa bit the inside of her lip. 'You don't have to… Stick around if you don't have anything better to do.'

Thank her for a good time, kiss her goodbye and walk on out…

'Thanks, I'll do that.'

His sensible side cursed him a blue streak for staying exactly where he was and stalked off. Since Patrick—his cousin, partner and accountant, who'd accompanied him from South Africa to work on establishing their companies here—was spending the weekend with an old university friend, Rob rationalised, why should he spend the day alone? He liked people, and they, despite the fact that he could be blunt and frequently tactless, liked him. So Rob thought he might as well hang around… He could always change his mind and leave. That was one of the cool benefits of free will.

He folded his arms against his chest and his biceps stretched the fabric of his creased shirt. He kept his eyes and tone inscrutable. 'So, apparently this house is part of your divorce settlement? You are still technically married.'

Willa sent him an uncertain look and for a moment she looked a lot younger and a great deal more vulnerable than he'd expected. His heart shuddered and he told it to get a grip... He wasn't a sap about women and their wobbly lips and soft eyes.

'We've been separated, officially, for a little more than half a year; in reality we haven't had a marriage for more years than I can count. Should I have told you?' she asked, unscrewing and then replacing the cap of her mascara in a movement that suggested OCD or nervousness.

If she had mentioned the M-word in the bar he would have run as fast and as far as he could, not even sticking around long enough to hear that she was separated. Was he crazy about the fact that she was still married? No. Was it going to stop him from sleeping with her again? Hell, no.

'I don't sleep with married women,' he stated, and wasn't sure if he was informing her or reminding himself.

Willa met his gaze in the mirror and her aqua eyes were direct and honest. She tossed the tube of mascara onto the counter and slapped her hands on her hips. 'I don't cheat. I haven't slept with anyone else and I would not have slept with you if I'd still felt morally married.'

Rob lifted his hands, slightly amused at her spirited reply. 'Easy there, tiger.'

Willa glared at him. 'So, would *you* cheat if you were married?'

Of course not. But it was a moot point because he had no plans to get married—he couldn't, because marriage meant that he had to trust himself and his judgement when it came to women. And people.

Not gonna happen.

'Well? Would you? *Do* you?' Willa demanded, pulling

him back to this house, on another continent, a lifetime later.

'Sorry—missed that. What did you say?'

'Would you cheat on your wife? On your girlfriend? Is that something you already do?' There was no judgement in her voice, just curiosity.

'What? Cheat?' Rob twisted his lips. 'I'm single, and I don't get involved with anybody long enough for the question to arise.'

Willa released a long, surprised sigh. 'God, you're honest. I haven't met an honest man in a long, long time.'

'You've been hanging around with the wrong crowd, gorgeous; it's the only way to be,' Rob stated. 'So, in the spirit of honesty...do you want to do this again?'

He really didn't want her to say no, Rob realised. He wanted to make love to her again... If she didn't have a house full of people downstairs he'd lift her up onto that counter, spread her legs and pull her panties out of the way. He'd be inside her in a matter of seconds...

And there he went, rising in anticipation.

'You're talking about having sex again?'

At least she hadn't called it *making love*; if she had, he'd have had to correct her.

'Yeah. You keen? Pure sex, pure fun, no obligations or strings.'

'For how long?'

He wasn't idiot enough to make promises he couldn't keep. 'I have no freakin' idea. Once more? Twice? Sixteen times? I don't know...let's just play it by ear.'

Willa was so still and so quiet for such a long time that Rob thought she was about to say no and his heart plummeted. As earlier suggested: *Get a freakin' grip, dammit!*

'Yeah,' Willa said eventually. 'We can do that. Play it by ear.'

'Excellent.'

Rob slowly slowly, put his cup on the shelf next to the door and walked into the bathroom. Then he gripped her hips and easily lifted her up onto the bathroom counter, placing her between the two basins.

'Let's start right now.'

Since she'd just placed her hands on his chest and sucked his lower lip between her teeth, Rob assumed that she had no objections to his suggestion.

When Willa finally made it downstairs and stepped onto the outside entertainment area, still cross-eyed and lost in a lustful funk—she had a lover...*whoo!*—it felt as if she had been transported back eight years to the magical Whitsundays and the Weeping Reef resort. It was in the laughter she heard, the excitement in the voices of her guests, the rhythm of their speech.

She pulled in her breath and allowed the years to roll back to when she'd felt free and happy and sexy and... *happy*. Back then she'd thought that nothing bad could ever happen...and then it had. Amy was attacked and Scott and Brodie's friendship had blown up and everything changed.

She didn't respond well to change or to pain, and her distress that her friends had been hurting, that their magical time on the Whitsundays had ended so brutally, had just pushed her further into the arms of the older, romantic, tell-her-exactly-what-she-needed-to-hear Wayne. She'd felt safe there—cosseted, protected. After all, she'd been shielded from the vagaries of life since she was thirteen by her father, who didn't see why her being an adult should change that.

Note to Dad: life doesn't work that way.

Willa shook off her memories, put a smile on her face and ignored the flutter of nerves in her stomach. Nobody was judging her, waiting for her to fail, she told herself as she was recognised, as conversations were muted and a cluster of her old friends walked over to greet her.

'Oh, it's so good to see you.'

'You look fantastic.'

'Thank you for coming… Have a drink…help yourself to food.'

Willa kissed and hugged her guests, making her way across the veranda, and then Scott was standing in front of her, his arms open wide. Willa gave a cry of delight, stepped into his arms and Scott picked her up and swung her around. She could feel the strength in his arms, the power of his chest. His fabulous green eyes sparkled down at her and he smelled terrific. He was sexy and solid… But, nope, he didn't make her heart or her hormones hop.

'Scott, it's been so long!' she cried, and kissed his cheek.

'Looking good, Wills,' Scott said in his drawling voice, before stepping back to jam his hands into the pockets of his cargo shorts.

Willa, seeing Jessica standing next to Scott, and remembering that, without her help she'd be buzzing around like a demented fly, reached over and squeezed her arm. 'Thanks for setting everything out, Jess.'

'No worries.'

Amy's flatmate, wearing very dark glasses, was nursing what looked like a Bloody Mary. Jeez, she could do with one of those… Her booze hangover was gone, but she suspected that she now had a hangover thanks to too much sex. Don't get her wrong, she wasn't complaining…

Talking of spectacular sex… She turned around and saw Rob helping himself to a beer. 'And this is Rob…'

'Rob Hanson.'

Rob held his hand out for Scott to shake and within minutes was enveloped in his and Jessica's conversation. Seeing that her brand-new lover didn't need babysitting—

thank goodness—Willa sent him a slow smile and turned away to catch up with her friends.

While she played host, gently flirted with her old male friends and caught up with her old girlfriends, she exchanged hot looks with Rob. Even though he was still dressed in last night's jeans and shirt, he looked as if he'd stepped off the cover of a men's magazine. Broad shoulders, long legs, white teeth, and those silver eyes slightly shadowed by blue.

Willa couldn't believe that out of all those sexy girls in the club last night he'd come home with her—that he still wanted more from her. Again, she wasn't complaining… *at all*. She was just surprised and grateful.

Grateful that he was nice and fun and, yeah, *hard*. Skilled…hot.

Willa's conversation with Jane—if she could call Jane's wittering on about pottery classes and her not hearing a word a conversation—was interrupted when Amy grabbed her arm and whirled her away.

Willa sent Jane an apologetic smile but allowed Amy to pull her into a quiet corner. Remembering how curious Amy could be, she waited with lifted brows.

'How long does it take you to shower—or did you get distracted by the good-looking bloke with the funny accent?'

'He doesn't have a funny accent,' Willa protested, hoping to deflect Amy's nosiness.

'*Pfft.* We both know that I'm asking if you got shagged again,' Amy demanded.

'Ames, that's none of your…' Willa looked around and dropped her voice. 'Okay, I did. Again. On the counter of the bathroom and it was *fabulous*.'

'We can all tell,' Amy said dryly. Her expression changed and became a lot more sober. 'Look, I know I sort of pushed you towards him last night, but I thought you'd just flirt

with him and it would cheer you up. All this... Well, do
you know what you're doing, Wills? He's a nice guy, but
he has short-term written all over him.'

Eight years on and she was being shooed away under
Amy's wing again. Willa rubbed her shoulder with her
hand, thinking that she was a big girl and didn't need to
be shooed anywhere any more.

'So he told me. Relax, Ames, I'd be an idiot if I fell for
the first man I had sex with after The Pain, and I really am
trying not to be an idiot about men any more.'

'Promise?'

'That I'm not going to be an idiot? Well, I promise to
try...' Willa smiled. 'So, what are we eating? Drinking?'

Amy gestured to the dining table, piled high with sal-
ads, a couple of loaves of fresh bread and various dips. 'I
bought enough to feed an army. There are prawns and cray-
fish in the fridge that the boys can throw on the barbie...
wine, beer, coolers to drink.'

Willa looked from the food to her friend. 'You need to
tell me what I owe you.'

'Later.'

'Can you believe how many people came? It's amazing...'

'You were always a lot more popular than you realised,
Willa,' Amy replied. 'I just wish...'

'That Luke and Brodie and Chantal were here?' Willa
finished her sentence. 'Me too.' She took Amy's hand.
'Thank you for doing the food—thank you for making me
do this. I feel like the others are just around the corner...
like we're waiting for them to arrive.'

'Me too.' Amy looked down at their clasped hands and
licked her lips. 'Talking of friends... Did I ever say thanks,
Willa? For helping me that night? For picking me up and
patching me up?'

Willa looked at the faint scar just below Amy's eye and

acid rolled through her stomach. 'God, I am just so glad that he didn't…you know…'

'Rape me? Yeah, me too. Though he packed a pretty mean punch,' Amy said in a low, bitter tone. 'If it wasn't for you—for Luke—I don't know if I could've got through that night.'

'I wish you hadn't left, Amy. It wasn't the same without you.'

Amy shook her head. 'Honey, how could I stay? I was front of house and I looked like a raccoon, with two black and blue eyes, a split cheek and a fat lip. I couldn't work like that, I didn't want to answer questions from our friends and I couldn't tolerate the idea of seeing Justin again.'

'Luke kicked him off the property and told him never to return. I suspected he also might have punched him… I saw that his knuckles were a bit sore and raw for a couple of days after you left.'

Amy's eyes softened. 'That Luke. I was crazy about him. I only went to the beach with Justin in an attempt to make Luke feel jealous.' Amy looked out onto the harbour. 'Is he okay, Willa? Really?'

Oh, hell, how did she answer that? 'Oh, Ames, I don't know. We're not that close, and he'd never talk to his younger sister if something was worrying him.'

Amy tilted her head. 'Why not?'

'I was thirteen when my mum died and it messed me up. Messed *us* up. Dad wrapped me in cotton wool, and then in bubble wrap, but he left Luke to flounder.'

'I don't understand.'

Hell, she didn't either.

'Luke dealt with Mum's death on his own. Maybe it was because he was older and a young adult already, away at uni, but Dad cosseted me and pretty much ignored Luke. It created a distance between us.'

Her father hadn't done them any favours… She'd grown

up to be spoilt and naïve and Luke had remained on the outside of a family circle reduced to two. She still felt guilty
about that, and wished that her father had handled the situation—them—differently. Wished that he'd allowed her to
grow up and make some mistakes, allowed Luke to grieve
with them instead of encouraging him to work and study
his way through his pain.

As a result she'd come to believe that all she needed was
a strong man to sort her problems out and protect her from
the nasties life could throw her way. Luke had become a
highly self-sufficient and extremely independent businessman, with an inability to become emotionally engaged.

'What are you trying to tell me, Willa?'

*Don't pin your hopes on him; find a nice man who will
love you with everything he has. Luke is too complicated,
too self-sufficient, too distant.*

Willa started to say the words and then shook her head.
The heart wanted what the heart wanted, and nothing she
could say would have any effect. And for all she knew she
could be barking up the wrong tree.

Willa snagged a cold beer from the fridge and lifted her
shoulders in a what-the-hell-do-I know? shrug. 'I don't have
a clue, Ames. Ignore me.'

Later that afternoon Willa, with Scott, Rob and Amy, sat
at the round wooden table at the far end of the pool, under
the shade of a large umbrella. Her other guests—including
Jessica, who'd caught a ride with one of the old Whitsundays lifeguards…cute, but not a rocket scientist!—had all
left, and the four of them were lazily picking at a selection
of snacks as a late-afternoon treat.

Amy leaned across the table and lightly touched Scott's
arm. 'I haven't had a chance to speak to you, Scott, and I
want to catch up with what's going on in your life. Willa
says that you're an architect.'

'Yep.'

'And how's Chantal?'

Willa sucked in a deep breath and winced. With all the craziness she hadn't had time to fill Amy in on exactly what had happened after she'd left the Weeping Reef. 'Uh, Ames...'

Amy ignored her interruption. 'She's not here with you... why not? Are you two still together?'

Scott stared hard at his beer bottle. 'No, we broke up,' he answered eventually.

'When?' Amy demanded.

'How are your folks, Amy?' Willa asked, desperately hoping to change the subject.

Amy waved her question away. 'Fine. I really wish she and Brodie were here. Okay, you obviously don't want to talk about Chantal. Then tell me about Brodie, Scott. How is he? *Where* is he?'

Willa groaned. *Shoot me now.*

Scott smiled thinly, drained his beer, stood up and held out his hand for Rob to shake. He bent down and kissed Willa's cheek. 'Thanks for a great day, Willa. Let's get together again and catch up.'

'No, don't go,' Willa said.

Scott's smile didn't reach his eyes. 'I need to get moving. You stay and tell Miss Curiosity, here—' he ruffled Amy's hair '—about the last episode of the soap opera that was the Weeping Reef.' He lifted his hand and shook his head. 'No, don't get up—I'll let myself out.'

Willa felt sad as she watched Scott walk away. He was such a good guy, but the situation with Brodie and Chantal, old as it was, obviously still bugged him.

She turned to Amy and sighed. 'Well, didn't *you* put your foot in it?'

'In what?' Amy asked, looking around, her expression pure confusion. 'What did I say?'

'I keep forgetting that you weren't there when it all happened…' Willa mused.

'*What* happened?' Amy demanded.

Willa took a breath, leaned back in her seat and rewound. Scott and Chantal: the golden couple of the resort. Scott the head sailing instructor, and perky, talented Chantal—Head of Entertainment—had been an item, and everyone had assumed that they were perfect for each other. No one except her had seemed to notice the sexual tension between Chantal and Brodie, Scott's fellow sailing instructor and his best friend.

It had been a recipe for disaster and it had exploded in their faces the night after Amy had left town.

It had taken one song, one slow dance between Scott's girlfriend and his best friend, for Scott—and everyone else in the room—to see that they both wanted to get naked very, very soon. With each other. The sexual tension and electricity had crackled around them as they'd danced, seemingly oblivious to the fact that everyone—and Scott—was watching them. The song had ended and so had their friendship…

Scott's fist had connected with Brodie's face—resulting in the second black eye in consecutive days—and wild accusations had bounced off the walls. Willa knew that nothing had happened between Scott and Chantal except for excessive heat, but Scott had felt betrayed and Brodie guilty, because he'd firmly subscribed to the notion of 'mates before pretty much everything else'.

Brodie had left and Chantal had walked around as a shadow of her former perky self. Her remaining weeks at the resort, *sans* Amy and Brodie, had been miserable—as Willa now told Amy

When she was finished Amy shook her head. 'But that's stupid,' she stated. 'They only danced! That wasn't a good enough reason to break up—for Brodie and Scott to fight.'

'Yeah, it was,' Rob said quietly. When both pairs of feminine eyes landed on his face he shrugged. 'Guy dances with his best mate's girl and looks like he wants to do her—best mate has grounds to be pissed off. Big-time.'

Amy looked scornful. 'But he didn't *do* anything!'

'It doesn't matter. It was a metaphorical kick to Scott's balls…' Rob rolled his beer bottle between the palms of his hands. 'Did Brodie hit Scott back?'

Willa shook her head. 'No, he just stood there, taking it. Then he walked away and just…left.'

Rob nodded. 'Sounds about right.'

This all seemed very natural and normal to him… Willa pulled her eyebrows together. Were she and Amy missing something critical here? Some subtle male nuance that had completely escaped them because they lacked testosterone and masculine bits and bobs?

'But they haven't spoken for eight years!' Willa protested.

'They'll talk when they're ready to…or not.' Rob stated. 'My advice? Stay out of it.'

Like Amy, Willa just stared at him.

Willa eventually sighed and shook her head. 'Boys are just weird.'

CHAPTER FOUR

AMY, FED, WATERED and out of reminiscences, didn't leave until after six that evening and Willa was exhausted. Her house looked as if a bomb had hit it, and she groaned at the thought of clearing up; she just wanted to climb into a shower and then into her bed.

She stepped into her hall, looked at those steep, floating stairs, walked over to them and sat down on the bottom step. Rob hadn't left yet, and she wasn't sure how she felt about that. Part of her desperately wanted to be alone, to process the fact that in the space of twenty-four hours she'd had her first one-night stand *and* reconnected with most of her friends from Weeping Reef. She was very used to being alone—not so much to having so many people in her space.

'Willa…?'

Willa looked up and smiled at Rob, who'd come into the hall, holding his mobile in his hand. 'Sorry, I just sat down for a moment.'

'You must be exhausted. I know I am.' Rob sat down on the stair next to her. 'I've called for a taxi. It'll be here soon.'

'You don't need to leave…' Willa protested, innately polite but secretly relieved.

Rob briefly touched her hand with his. 'Yeah, I think I do. Neither of us got much sleep last night and it's been a long day.'

Willa picked at the frayed cotton on the hem of her denim shorts. 'I had fun.'

'I imagine that reconnecting with your friends has brought back a truckload of memories,' Rob commented.

Willa smiled. 'Some good, some that make me cringe, or laugh, and others that make me want to cry.'

'Where *are* the...?' Rob snapped his fingers. 'I can't remember the name of the place you met them.'

'The Whitsundays? It's a group of islands in the heart of the Great Barrier Reef.'

'Tell me about them,' Rob commanded gently.

Willa placed her chin in the palm of her hand and her eyes went soft and dreamy. 'Jeez, where do I start? Brilliant sunsets, white sands, fantastic shades of clear water. I dived and snorkelled whenever I could—I was absolutely fascinated by the fish and corals. There's a coral called the weeping coral—that's where the resort we all worked at got its name.'

'And you looked after kids?'

'Yeah, I loved running the kids' activity programme. It filled the days—and at night we partied. Amy taught me to flirt—well, she tried to—and to party. I fell well short of her legendary standards. But I learnt to hold my drink and—as much as I could—to cut loose. I...blossomed.'

'You met your husband there?'

Willa nodded a little forlornly. 'He was older, wiser, and to me—being from a small town where everyone knew, loved and protected me—he seemed so refined. Charisma, confidence and charm. Being noticed by Wayne was a huge ego boost, and after I realised that he was actually interested in me I felt sophisticated and special.'

'As you would.'

She'd tumbled into love with him. In hindsight, she'd probably been more in love with the way he'd made her feel—strong, sexy and stylish. Amy had thought Wayne was too flash, too demanding, and Luke had questioned what a thirty-three-year-old man saw in his country bumpkin teenage sister, but she'd brushed their concerns away... She'd been in love and she'd felt marvellous.

'I was eighteen years old and I thought I knew what I was doing and nobody was going to spoil it for me.' *Yeah, right.*

'I have a theory that there should be a law against anyone making life-changing decisions before they're twenty five.'

Willa picked up the sour note in his voice and tipped her head. 'Did you make some bad choices too?'

'You have no idea.' Rob gestured for her to continue her story. 'Carry on.'

'Something bad happened to Amy that made her leave the resort, and then there was the blow-up between Chantal, Scott and Brodie. I shoved my head into the sand and started spending more and more time with Wayne.'

The dissent at the resort had shoved her further into Wayne's arms... She'd felt safe there, and protected. When she'd been with him she'd had a break from worrying about Amy, and she'd been able to escape the tension between Chantal and Scott.

'At the end of the season he proposed and I accepted. I was marrying a gorgeous, romantic older guy, who would love and take care of me for the rest of my life. What could possibly go wrong?'

'Things obviously did?'

'Yeah—big-time.'

Rob didn't push for more and she appreciated his tact. She'd said more than she'd meant to and she couldn't explain that while there had been love, it had been a distorted version of the emotion. Love on his terms. He'd taken care of her financially, not emotionally, and cheated on her constantly.

His had been a love that was rude, conditional, disparaging. Controlling. That was why she was embarking on this short-term fling with Rob—it was healthy, a positive step in the rehabilitation of Willa. It was honest, it was temporary, it was…straightforward. Direct, undemanding, clear-cut. It was everything she'd never had with Wayne…

And the sex—well, that was nothing like she'd had with her ex. Just the thought of Rob's hot, muscled body made her mouth dry up; she felt tingly and dizzy, feminine and free.

This was the way she'd felt that summer at Weeping Reef—before all the drama. Strong, healthy, sexy…free. Her freedom had been taken away for eight years, but she was not going to waste a second of it now.

Rob spun his mobile around on the palm of his hand with his finger. 'So, you're still okay with the no-strings sex decision we made earlier?'

There was that in-your-face honesty again. God, she loved it. 'Yes.'

Rob placed his hand on her slim thigh and squeezed. 'Good. I'll call you.'

'You don't have my number,' Willa pointed out, leaning her elbows on the step behind her.

'I found your phone and dialled my number—saved my number to your contacts,' Rob explained on an easy grin. 'You don't have that many contacts on your phone, so I should be easy enough to find.'

'I figured that if I didn't have to talk to my ex then I sure didn't have to talk to his snooty friends either. Another of the many benefits of getting divorced. Can I ask you a favour?' she asked, looking at his strong profile.

'Mmm? What?'

'On the day the divorce becomes final, if you are still around, will you help me celebrate by doing something completely wild with me?'

Rob tipped his head. 'Like…?'

'Like a motorbike ride, or bungee-jumping, or sky-diving… Flying to the Whitsundays for a couple of days and doing a wreck dive—I'll pay. I want do something that makes me feel crazily alive and free, and I think you might be the type of guy who would be up for doing that with me.'

'What do *I* get out of it?' Rob asked, his mouth twitching in amusement.

'Um...crazy sex?' Willa suggested.

'Oh, I intend having crazy sex with you anyway.'

Rob picked up her hand and kissed her open palm, his fabulous eyes hot and heated as they connected with hers.

'Sure, I'll help you celebrate your freedom, Willa. Let me know the day and we'll do something to mark the occasion.'

Rob leaned forward and brushed her lips with his and Willa's heart sighed. His kiss was gentle and sexy—a nibble here, a lick there. It was as if he knew he couldn't take it deeper or further, that they were out of time...for now.

And they were. They had barely started when they heard the toot of a taxi horn.

Rob pulled away and stood up, jamming his hands into the pockets of his jeans. 'I'm going to go...get some sleep. And, Willa?'

'Mmm?'

'The phone works both ways.' Rob waggled his eyebrows. 'You need me for a booty call—don't be shy.'

Willa grinned. 'I might take you up on that.'

'Feel free.'

After kissing Willa's cheek, Amy slid into a chair on the other side of the small table in the outside shaded seating area of Saints, which morphed into a trendy bistro during the day. Amy pushed her designer sunglasses up into her hair and scanned the specials board, quickly ordering a frappe and a goat's cheese salad from the hovering waiter—whose knees, Willa was sure, buckled under the force of her smile.

'Sorry, I'm late. I was in a meeting with Rob.'

Willa, who hadn't heard from Rob since he'd left her house on Sunday, tried not to sound too eager. 'Oh…?'

'Poor guy is looking a bit frazzled. I told him we were meeting for lunch.'

And did he have anything to say to that? Willa growled her frustration as Amy picked up her phone, checked her messages and smiled at a cute guy who was walking past. Ah, this was vintage Amy, who could be annoying as all hell.

Willa picked up her fork and not so gently poked the back of Amy's hand with the tines.

Amy attempted to look innocent, but since the last time she'd been innocent had been when she was in utero, she didn't quite pull it off. 'Oh, you want to know if he gave any reaction…?'

Willa growled again, and lifted the fork in a threatening movement.

'How old did you say you are again?' Amy asked. 'Fifteen?'

Willa sighed and drew patterns on the colourful tablecloth with the fork. 'I know. I'm such a dork.'

Amy laughed and held up her hands in surrender. 'He said that if you asked I was to remind him of your last conversation… Which means what?'

The phone works both ways…booty call.

Willa explained.

'He's right,' Amy said. 'But he doesn't know that you would rather chop off your own head than risk being rejected…'

Willa glared at her. 'I am not eighteen any more!'

'Then call him—tell him you're horny and you want him bad,' Amy challenged her, one eyebrow raised.

Willa felt her neck and cheeks heat up. Hell, she couldn't do that—could she?

'As you said…you are such a dork,' Amy said, with absolutely no malice in her voice. 'Newsflash, honey: girls are allowed to ask boys out.'

'Asking someone out on a date is a bit different from asking someone to come over and take you to bed,' Willa protested.

'Why? It's the twenty-first century.' Amy took the fork from her hand and set it on the table, waited for Willa to meet her eyes. 'That being said, you *are* playing it cool with him, aren't you, Willa?'

'Of course I'm playing it cool, Amy—not that I have much choice. Rob is unfailingly honest—haven't you noticed? I know exactly where I stand and I'm very comfortable being his sex-with-no-strings girl.'

'Okay, as long as you know what you're doing.' Amy grinned. 'He *is* honest, isn't he? Today he told the director of marketing—my boss—that his ideas were crap and that he was paying them for my expertise not his. Since the director has the marketing smarts of a moose, and is only there because he married the owner's daughter, I was cheering. But the sensible part of me remembered that he's my boss, so it was only on the inside! Anyway, are you going to call him?'

'No.'

'Cluck-cluck.'

Willa rolled her eyes. 'You're not going to dare me into making a booty call, Amy.'

Amy said nothing and lounged in her chair, her eyes laughing.

'I'm okay with being a dork, a wuss, a chicken,' Willa protested.

Amy used the same look she'd used to get her to do all those things they shouldn't have as staff members at the Weeping Reef Resort. Skinny-dipping and raiding the kitchen for late-night snacks had been minor transgressions. Doing golf cart doughnuts on the greens of the golf course had been a major misdemeanour—amongst others.

Amy would just wait her out until Willa did what she wanted her to do… Hell, when Willa did what she herself wanted to do. She wanted Rob back in her bed, back inside her, making her eyes cross with pleasure.

Huffing a frustrated sigh, she dug in her bag for her mobile and found the number she now knew by heart.

'Gorgeous,' Rob said, after answering on the second ring.

And that one word and his amused voice gave her courage.

'Booty call,' she whispered softly, ignoring Amy's triumphant grin.

'Tied up until late tonight,' Rob answered, just as briefly. 'I can be there around eleven.'

'I'll be up.'

Willa disconnected and held up a finger. 'Not one word!'

'Not one word except that I am mega impressed. Short, succinct, direct,' Amy said cheerfully. 'Okay, that was a whole bunch of words. Changing the subject…. I love your shoes.'

Willa looked down at her strappy high-heeled sandals. 'I'd like them more if I'd paid for them… I need a job, Amy. I need to *do* something.'

'You've got your degree, Wills, and you've got a Masters! Surely there must openings somewhere?' Amy sat back as the waiter placed her iced coffee in front of her.

Willa sighed. 'I was offered a job about two months ago—a really nice position with a new clothing brand—but Kate didn't want me to take it in case it jeopardised my divorce claim. I kept telling her that I'd rather have the job than the money, but she advised me to sit tight.'

'I'd like to meet her,' Amy said. 'She sounds nice.'

'She really is—and she's a damn good lawyer. I want

to be her when I grow up. She's a high-achieving, competent and highly confident woman—she definitely doesn't need a man. That being said, she does get very protective over her clients… You should have seen her wipe the floor with Wayne's smug attitude. She had him tied up in knots—his lawyer too.'

Amy smiled in appreciation. 'Just for that she has my unending appreciation. Anyway, getting back to you and a job…have you applied anywhere else?'

'I haven't seen any openings and I've been looking. I think the type of accounting job I'm aiming for needs experience, or contacts, or a network—or something else that I don't have. I'm *good*, Ames—or at least I could be good if someone gave me a damn chance,' Willa replied bitterly. 'I just feel so…useless. I sneaked around for years, getting that cursed degree, and nobody seems to want to see me put it to use!'

'I take it The Pain wasn't exactly supportive of your studying?'

Willa snorted.

She'd begged Wayne to allow her to study but he'd laughed away her ambitions. Even if he had said yes she'd known that keeping up with her course work while following her husband around the world like a lapdog would be impossible.

It had only been when Wayne had started leaving her at home in their luxury penthouse apartment—probably around the time he'd engaged in his first affair—that she'd signed up for an online degree and studied in secret, knowing how dismissive and cruel Wayne could be. There had simply been no point in giving him more ammunition to take pot-shots at her…

When he'd found her graduation papers, hidden under the lavender-scented drawer lining of her lingerie drawer—why he'd been looking in her panty drawer still boggled the brain—he'd been, as she'd suspected, completely dismissive, belittling her dreams of having any type of professional career, and also furious because she'd pulled the wool over his eyes.

That argument—and the fact that he'd had smudged lipstick on his jawline—had been the final straw, the last nail in the coffin, the excuse she'd been looking for to walk away from him...and to keep on walking, straight into a lawyer's office.

'No, he wasn't supportive. Anyway, let's not talk about him. But if you hear of anything will you let me know?'

'Sure. So, I had a drink with Scott and he told me that you guys met for coffee yesterday?'

'We did. And Brodie sent me a message apologising for not making the party. He's invited us both out to lunch next week as he's in Sydney.'

'But he didn't invite Scott?'

Willa's chest lifted in frustration. 'Nope. Anyway, I looked at Brodie's photos online and, while he was always a good-looking guy, it looks like he's lifted *sexy* to a whole new level. So has Scott, actually.'

'I know. I thought that too,' Amy replied, wrinkling her nose. 'But the thought of doing either of them is like...'

'Creepy? Incesty?'

'Yeah—that! I feel like I'm perving over my brother!' Amy looked relieved. 'I thought it was only me...I'm glad you feel the same.'

'Maybe it's got something to do with the fact that we've seen them snot-drunk and puking?' Willa mused, but knew that, for her, it was more the fact that neither of them—good-looking devils that they were—could hold a candle to the man who'd shared her bed on Saturday night. Who'd share her bed tonight...

And she suspected that, for Amy, neither of them

matched up to a certain man in Singapore who was also her brother.

Dammit.

The doorbell rang at about eleven-thirty and Willa put her hand on her stomach as she left the library and walked down the passage to the hall. She was dressed in a brief T-shirt and briefer denim shorts and her feet were bare... This was a booty call and she hadn't bothered to dress up— mostly because she wanted to get naked as soon as possible.

Willa opened the front door and there he was, standing beneath the porch light. Her heart bounced off a rib and she licked her lips, looking for any moisture she could find. In a pair of smart grey suit pants, a pale blue shirt and grey tie, he looked tall, rangy, fit...businesslike.

Willa connected with his eyes and sighed... Along with lust—and there was a lot of that in his eyes—she saw frustration and stress and a whole bunch of exhausted.

'Hey...' she murmured, grabbing his tie and pulling him inside.

'Hey back.' Rob put his hands on her hips, his thumbs skimming the strip of bare skin between her shorts and T-shirt. But instead of kissing her, he laid his forehead on hers and sighed.

Willa hooked her hand abound the back of his neck and felt the tension in his rock-hard muscles. 'Bad day?'

'Frustrating rather than bad. Sorry I'm late.'

'No worries. Want a drink?'

Willa took his hand and led him to the kitchen, directing him to a bar stool before opening the fridge door and pulling out a bottle of wine.

Rob wrinkled his nose. 'Light, calorie-free wine? Got any whisky?'

'Sure.'

Willa replaced the wine and turned to a cupboard next to

the fridge. She pulled out a bottle of Macallan and swore she heard Rob groan in appreciation. Pouring two fingers into a tumbler, she added ice and handed it over. Rob sipped, closed his eyes, and rested the glass against his forehead.

The man was exhausted, Willa realised. The shadows she'd seen under his eyes at the weekend were now solid purple stripes. He'd scraped the scruff off his face, but she could see stress in his hard jaw, in the deepening of the fine lines around his face.

'You okay, Rob?'

Rob ran a hand across his face. 'Yeah, sorry...little distracted. It's been a couple of long, tense, tough days.'

'Any particular reason?'

'Just the normal stress when you're trying to set up a business in a foreign country. The rand also weakened substantially today, which shrinks our capital.'

His days had been more than difficult—they'd been brutal. She could tell by the stress in his shoulders, the banked anger, the waves of frustration.

'We don't have to do this tonight. If you'd rather go... do.' Willa licked her lips. 'Don't feel like you have to stay.'

Rob put his glass down on the granite counter-top, leaned forward and hooked his finger in the V of her shirt, pulling her gently towards him. 'There's nowhere else I'd rather be. I've been thinking of you, remembering you... under me, wet and warm...every night and a whole lot during the day. Sexy daydreams of you have been hell on my productivity.'

Well, then... Okay...

Rob's hands skimmed up her sides and his thumbs whispered over her breasts—a teasing hint of pleasure to come. Willa felt warm, moist lust between her legs as she stepped between Rob's open thighs, almost swallowing her tongue at the sight of the long, thick ridge in his pants.

'I need to be inside you,' Rob muttered, his mouth against her neck, making her shiver.

Willa pulled his tie, then left it loose as she worked to undo the buttons on his shirt. Then she pulled his shirt apart and placed her hands on his warm, masculine skin. She could smell his deodorant, soap, and warm, excited, turned-on male.

'I need you to be inside me.' Willa told him, scraping her nails across his flat nipples, down his ribcage and over his ridged abdominal muscles.

And she did. She'd never felt quite as alive, as fulfilled, as she had when Rob had been inside her, rocking her into oblivion. Willa dropped her hand over his crotch and lightly cupped him. She tipped her head back to smile into his eyes before stepping away from him and holding out her hand.

When he stood and enveloped her hand in his much broader, stronger one she sent him a slow smile. 'Come to bed and let's get naked.'

Rob's eyes lightened and he flashed her one of his devastating grins. 'You really are getting the hang of this booty call stuff.'

Setting up a business in a foreign country was a pain, Rob thought, pressing the doorbell of Willa's idiotically big house, and it was full of stupidities and intricacies that he didn't find back home. So why, instead of working his way through the pile of documents that sat on the desk— as Patrick was doing at the moment, in the two-bedroomed apartment he'd rented in the city—was he standing here hoping she'd open the door?

And why *wasn't* she opening the door? he wondered, looking around. Her little Mercedes sat in the driveway and he could hear music—hard rock and loud—coming from somewhere inside the house.

Turning the knob on the door, he frowned when it

opened soundlessly. Burglars? Rapists? Murderers? *Willa...
haven't you heard of those?* He walked into the massive
hall, deliberately ignoring the green monstrosity that called
itself art on the wall.

Rob left the keys to the SUV he'd rented and his wal-
let and mobile on the hall table, made sure that the front
door was locked, and then walked through the house in the
direction of the music, looking into rooms as he walked
down the passage.

Massive reception room with heavy furniture and an
air of emptiness, a library/TV lounge that looked messy
and lived-in, and a formal dining room with a huge dining
table and more weird art.

The music was increasing in volume and he looked to his
right, where he saw a short flight of stairs. Walking down
them, he lifted his brows when he saw the fully equipped
gym downstairs. He whistled in appreciation at the up-to-
date equipment: she had most of what he intended to put
in *his* gyms.

A massive plasma screen TV covered half of one wall
and on the mat in front of it was a sweaty and puffy Willa—
dressed in the tiniest pair of gym shorts and a T-back
crop-top—trying to follow the instructions of a Tae Bo
instructor. Kick, punch, side kick...

Rob smiled, Willa was about as co-ordinated as a newly
born giraffe—all arms and legs heading in different directions.

Rob looked around, found the music system and hit the
'off' button. Willa whirled around at the silence. She caught
a glimpse of him and screamed, instinctively lifted a bar-
bell above her head.

Rob grinned and lifted up his hands. 'Relax, Wills, it's
me.'

Willa lowered the weight and glared at him. 'Thanks

bunches—you just took ten years off my life. Do you normally stroll into people's houses and scare them to death?'

'I wouldn't have strolled in at all if you hadn't left your front door unlocked! That's stupid!'

Willa tapped her foot on the exercise mat and he could see the irritation on her face.

'And do you normally stroll into people's houses with no notice and call them *stupid*?'

Rob nodded, acknowledging the criticism. She might have got married when she was a baby but she wasn't anyone's push-over—or at least not any more.

'Sorry…let's start again. Hi, how are you?'

He could see her debating whether she should give him more grief, but then her shoulders dropped and the moment passed.

'Hi back.' She ran her hand over her forehead and grimaced at her sweaty fingers. 'Yuck. Sorry—not at my freshest…'

'There's nothing wrong with a bit of sweat.' He looked around again. 'This is impressive, Willa. Did you buy the equipment?'

Willa picked up a gym towel and rubbed the back of her neck and her face. 'No, it all came with the house. Wayne-the-Pain bought the house shortly before we separated; the entire house and all its contents were up for auction. That's one of the things he does—snaps up properties for a song and resells them. He bought the place—all furniture, art, gym equipment included—and moved me into it until we finalised the divorce. Then I hired Kate as my lawyer and she decided that I should keep it as a sorry-I-cheated present.'

'Hell of a present,' Rob said, inspecting a brand-new, never-been-used rowing machine. 'So you don't use the equipment?'

'It intimidates the hell out of me,' Willa replied, heading for a small bar fridge and pulling out a bottle of water.

He nodded when she offered him one and caught the bottle she tossed in his direction with one hand. After cracking the lid and swallowing half the bottle, she nodded at the instructor on the big screen, who was still kicking and punching.

'I stick to Tae-Bo and Pilates. And I run.'

'I could show you how to use it properly if you'd like,' Rob suggested, moving to a treadmill and pressing the computer to see its functions. He whistled, impressed. It was top of the line and, again, unused. What a waste.

Willa walked back to the mat and sat down under the air-conditioning vent. 'Have you always been sporty?' she asked. 'Is that why you do what you do?'

Rob shot her a quick look, about to give her his stock answer—that he'd always been sporty and going into the fitness industry had been a natural progression for him. He *was* sporty, and it *had* been a natural progression for him. But his Uncle Sid's gym—that smelly, masculine environment—had been the place he'd run to after his dad died.

'My dad died when I was sixteen, I used to go to my uncle's gym with him. It was the place where I still felt connected to my dad.'

After his mum had split from Stefan, leaving him with an inability to trust and a zero tolerance for bullies, exercise had been the way he'd held the demons of guilt and recrimination at bay.

'My Uncle Sid wanted to retire, and when I had the opportunity to buy a half-share of his gym along with Patrick, his son, I jumped at the chance.'

And three years later he and Patrick had had a string of sports equipment and clothing stores and a handful of men-only gyms. Now, ten years later, they were expanding into Australia.

'And that was your first business?'

'Mmm. We kept the gym a men-only operation—kept it low-key and unpretentious but brilliantly equipped—and it started gaining a reputation as a place for serious athletes who paid less attention to how they looked and more attention to how they felt. We encourage our clients to be strong, healthy, balanced, fit—we don't support bodybuilding for the sake of bodybuilding.'

Rob lifted his eyes from the monitor to see Willa looking quizzically at him.

'I don't believe in it. I use the machines because they have a place in a workout, but I—and my staff—encourage our clients to use a range of exercise techniques. Martial arts, Pilates, running, swimming, boxing...'

Willa leaned back on her hands and stretched out her legs. 'I still don't think that opening another gym in today's market is a good idea.'

Rob swung the punchbag as he moved over to the mat and sat down next to her. 'You need to stretch or else you're going to stiffen up.'

He waited until Willa had grabbed her toes and groaned as her muscles pulled.

'I have actually done some research, Willa,' he said mildly. 'I've visited a number of the competition's gyms in various areas and, while they are suitable for daily use, the staff and the atmosphere don't work for a serious athlete. The people I am targeting for my three gyms are hardcore athletes—sportsmen who need more intensive training. My gyms come with personal trainers who are a class above; they can design programs tailored to individuals. I'll have physiotherapists and dieticians on the premises, biokinetics.'

Willa just looked at him and he could see the wheels in her head turning.

'Sounds expensive.'

'It *is* expensive, but market research tells me that there are many people—and sports organisations—willing and prepared to pay the price to get the results. There's a big gap in the market and I intend to fill it.'

'You sound confident,' Willa said, stretching her arms over her head.

Her breasts lifted and her nipples, easily discernible through her crop-top, pebbled. His mouth dried up and his shorts tightened.

'I am confident…if we get through the damn paperwork required to set up a business by a foreigner in your country.'

Willa's face brightened. 'I could help you with that.'

Yeah… Sorry, gorgeous, but I'm not trusting my brand-new business to someone with a degree but no experience. Even if *I* think you're smart…

'Patrick, my cousin, is an accountant, and he's here with me. He's sorting it out.'

'Okay.' Willa's lips twisted as she stood up, hurt flashing in her eyes.

Feeling as if he'd kicked her cat, and not sure why, Rob gently hooked his leg around her calves and tumbled her back down to the mat. She fell on her back, as he'd intended her to, and within seconds he was leaning over her, his hands on either side of her face.

Brushing her mouth with his—once, twice—he smiled. 'Want to fool around?'

He saw her intake of breath and watched as her neck and cheeks flushed at the memory of shared pleasure. Her eyes deepened with lust as her hands sneaked up under his shirt and skittered over his abs, around and down…

'I'm all sweaty,' Willa protested, but not very convincingly.

'I own gyms. Sweat doesn't scare me.' Rob grinned his pirate grin. 'And, honey, you're about to get a whole lot sweatier.'

CHAPTER FIVE

WILLA AND ROB were on the pier below her house. His feet were dangling in the warm waters of Parsley Bay, the sun was setting, and she was lying flat-out, her head resting on Rob's muscular thigh.

She looked up at him. His eyes were hidden behind wraparound sunglasses but he practically oozed testosterone. She was quite certain that if she looked closely she would be able to see it bubbling out from every pore. And it wasn't only his hard, muscular body that screamed it—he had a don't-mess-with-me attitude that melted women's panties and made men wary.

Yet he was, to all intents and purposes, still a stranger. It seemed strange that he could know her body so well, and she his, but she didn't even know the bare bones of his life.

'Where do you live in South Africa?'

Rob, his palms behind him on the deck, looked down at her. 'Jo'burg...Johannesburg,' he corrected. 'I live in a suburb called Sandton in our family home.'

Okay, he'd said that there was no significant other in his life, but she thought she'd check. 'Alone?'

'No, I live there with my six wives and ten kids,' Rob said wryly. 'Actually, I share the house with my younger sister Gail.'

'Parents?'

'My mum lives about ten minutes away. I told you that my dad died when I was a teenager.'

Willa knew that his hard-as-nails, don't-go-there voice was enough warning for anyone to back off and change the subject—but, strangely, Rob didn't intimidate her at all. He could be gruff and tactless and brutally honest but he was a straight-shooter. If he didn't want to talk, he wouldn't.

In case he felt like volunteering any more personal information she kept her eyebrows raised, pushing for more.

'Stop batting your eyelashes at me, Willa. Won't work.'

Rob brushed her hair from her face before putting his hand back on the deck. See, he could be all grumpy and grouchy and then he did something tender that blew her away.

She loved his tender...

Well, he didn't have to talk—but she could. And maybe her opening up would encourage him to do the same. So she sat up and sat cross-legged on the deck, facing his shoulder.

'My mum died when I was thirteen,' Willa said, after topping up their wine glasses. 'Brain aneurysm. One moment I had this perfect life and the next it was shattered. Luke, my brother, was at uni, so it was my dad and I. We lived in a small town, and everyone was *so* determined to make sure that nothing dreadful happened to me again.'

'Did that work for you?' Rob asked, bending one knee and resting his forearm on it.

'Nope—life doesn't work like that.' Willa flashed him a quick smile. 'I sort of believe that life is a series of lessons you are sent here to learn and no one can stop you learning them—no matter how hard they try.'

Intriguing, Rob thought. 'And what lessons have you been sent to learn?'

'Well, I haven't figured them all out yet, but I think that one of them is that I'm stronger than people thought I was. Stronger than *I* thought I was.'

'Explain.'

He sounded bossy, but Willa didn't mind. Rob wouldn't use ten words when one would do.

Willa was about to speak when she pulled back and

shook her head. No, she didn't think she would, thank you very much. Talking was a give and take affair, and if he wasn't prepared to reveal his secrets then neither would she.

'Another time,' Willa said, her voice resolute but not bitchy. She knew that he wouldn't push for more…she wasn't giving any man anything that she didn't get in return.

Besides, she reminded herself, this relationship was about fun and sex—not about probing each other's psyches.

'This is a beautiful spot, Wills,' Rob said, looking across the bay and the harbour towards the bridge.

'It is, isn't it?' Willa agreed as the setting sun hurled streaks of red and yellow across the sky. 'I'm not overly fond of the furnishings, but I love the house.'

'You didn't bring any stuff from your previous place?'

'Nothing to bring,' Willa explained. 'I have some furniture of my mum's that's in storage. Wayne wouldn't let me put it in our house because it didn't fit in with the vision of the interior designer.'

Rob muttered an expletive under his breath and Willa grinned.

'He is exactly that. Anyway, I'll use my mum's stuff when I know what I'm doing with this place.'

'Are you going to sell it?'

'Dunno. As I said—love the house, hate the furnishings. I don't *need* to sell it. Kate's negotiated me quite a settlement and I could live off that for a long, long time if I'm careful. Selling the house would mean that I could live very comfortably without ever lifting a finger, but I want a job—want to kick-start my career. I'm ten years behind everyone else—which is stupid because I *am* smart, dammit!'

'Never said you weren't,' Rob said, keeping his voice even. 'But what you are is inexperienced.'

'And how am I supposed to get some experience if no

one will give me a chance?' Willa cried. 'I'm so frustrated I could spit spiders.'

'You've just got to keep knocking on doors.'

'Easier said than done,' Willa muttered into her glass.

'It could be worse. You could be sitting in a crappy apartment, drinking cheap wine and eating a hunk of stale bread,' Rob pointed out.

'True. Did I start whining there?' Willa asked, cocking her head.

'It was close. And I don't do whining...it makes me impatient.'

'I think you're impatient anyway.'

'True enough,' Rob agreed, looking as if he was mulling an idea over in his head. 'You should sell the contents of the house if you hate them—the art has to be worth something—and keep the house if you like it. I'd be willing to make you an offer on the gym equipment you're not using.'

Willa frowned. 'Seriously? Why?'

'Because it's never been used and because it's top of the range—the latest models. You interested in that? I'd leave you with a couple of machines, after showing you how to use them correctly—the basics of what you'd need to train.'

Willa mulled his suggestion over. 'Let me think about it...talk to Kate. There's nothing I can do until I sign the papers anyway.'

'Do that,' Rob said. 'I'll put the offer down on paper in the meantime.'

'Yeah, okay... Kate would insist on that. She loves paper,' Willa said. 'I suppose I should get an art appraiser in.'

'Wouldn't hurt,' Rob replied. 'Sorry—won't make you an offer on the art; it's bloody ugly.'

'I think so too,' Willa agreed. 'And it gives me the creeps.' She drained her glass and, putting it down, whipped

her shirt off, revealing the top of a lime-coloured bikini.
'I'm going to swim. You coming?'

'Only if I can feel you up underwater.'

'I'm sure that that is one offer I *can* take you up on.'
Willa dropped her shorts and dived off the pier, surfac-
ing a long way away. 'Come on in—the water is divine!'

Rob pulled off his shirt, dropped his glasses and dived
into the bay, and Willa sighed in pleasure as he swam to
her, his long length cutting through the water with ease.
When he popped up next to her she looped her arms around
his neck and her legs around his waist.

Deciding that he was fit enough to tread water for both
of them, she brushed her lips against his, then again with
more heat as his hand slid beneath her bikini bottom and
covered one butt cheek.

Willa nipped his bottom lip and then soothed the bite
of pain away with her warm tongue. He immediately shot
up—zero to let's-get-naked in three seconds—and from
the glint in his eyes she knew that he wanted to haul her
back to shore and get her to a place where he could bury
himself, long and deep, inside her.

This was crazy, she thought, and wild. And because it
was so crazy, and so wild, it couldn't last.

Willa felt a pang somewhere in the region where her
heart resided and scoffed at herself.

*You don't need it to last, Moore-Fisher, you just need
to enjoy it.*

Enjoy him.

And that, she admitted as his mouth settled over hers
and he whirled her into another soul-scorching kiss, she
had no difficulty doing.

Rob and Patrick left the building housing Amy's marketing
company and stepped into the late-afternoon, still furnace-
hot sunshine. Yanking their sunglasses from their jacket

pockets, they slipped them over their eyes and immediately shrugged out of their suit jackets. Walking down the pavement to their rented SUV, which they'd miraculously found parking for two blocks down, they rolled up their shirt sleeves and yanked down their ties.

Rob was checking his mobile messages when his cousin's fist ploughed into his bicep.

'What the hell…?' Rob snapped his head up and glared at Patrick, who was pretending that he hadn't just sucker-punched him. 'What was that for?'

'That was for you wandering off into Never-Never Land and letting me answer all those marketing questions!' Patrick lifted his hand and pointed his thumb at his own chest. 'Me accounting—you marketing and sales and blowing smoke up people's butts.'

'I was there,' Rob protested, but without conviction.

He hadn't been, really. He'd spent most of the meeting staring at a picture on Amy's office wall. It had been of Willa and Amy, younger, plumper and a great deal happier, mugging it up for the camera. Willa's face radiated happiness and joy and a love of life. *That's how she should look all the time*, he'd thought.

Patrick's fist made him take a step sideways again, and he felt pins and needles rocket up his arm. He cursed Patrick roundly. 'What did I do *now*?' he demanded.

'Who are you? Freaking Peter Pan? You keep wafting away—dreaming of Tinkerbell, probably!' Patrick stopped as they approached the SUV and put his hands on his hips. 'Is this about the girl? The one you and Amy talked about before we started the meeting?'

'What girl?'

'Now he's going to be coy. The girl you've been sneaking out to see. The one whose bed you frequently sleep in. *That* girl, moron.'

Rob opened the car doors and they climbed inside. Rob immediately started the engine to get the air-con going.

'Willa—her name is Willa,' he finally admitted. He took a deep breath and jumped. 'Want to meet her?'

If he hadn't been so surprised at the words that had come out of his mouth he would have laughed at Patrick's bugged-out expression. Then his smart-ass cousin recovered and put a hand behind his ear.

'Sorry, run that by me again. Did you invite me to *meet her*?'

'More fool me,' Rob muttered.

'You *never* introduce me to your women. What's different about this one?'

There was a question he couldn't answer.

'I'm going to dinner and you're going back to the flat. I thought you might like to get out instead,' Rob stated as he adjusted the vents to get cold air blowing at his face.

Patrick called BS, as he'd known he would. Then he reached for his mobile and grinned gleefully. 'I've *got* to tell Heather about this.'

'You are such a girl,' Rob grumbled as he pulled out into the traffic. 'Willa is a woman I met. There's no need to get excited. It's food, some beers—that's it.'

'Followed by hot sex for you and for me Mrs Hand—'

Rob rocketed a fist into Patrick's shoulder. '*Blergh*. Thanks for the visual. Now I need to bleach my brain. Look, about Willa—we're just having a...a thing while I'm here.'

'A thing, huh? Well, that's got to be an improvement on one-night stands.'

'Don't get excited. She's not a keeper.'

'Is she hot?' Patrick demanded, before banging the side of his head with the flat of his hand. 'Sorry—stupid question. They are *always* hot.'

'Do you want to meet her or not?' Rob demanded, irritated.

'Hell, yeah.'

'Then shut the hell up and do *not* embarrass me at dinner. No stories about high school or university or anything else,' Rob threatened.

Although this conversation was *very* high school, he admitted.

Patrick grinned. 'You, the king of I-don't-care-what-anyone-thinks, wanting to make a good impression?' He lifted his mobile again, waving it around. 'Heather, baby, get your ice skates on—because hell just froze over!'

'I really don't know why Heather married you and not me. One of these days she's going to realise that you're a pain in the ass and she'll dump you for me,' Rob grumbled.

'You wish,' Patrick snapped back, but his face softened at the thought of his wife and four-year-old daughter.

Rob softened too; little Kiley was his goddaughter and the unofficial love of his life.

'Can I at least tell Willa about the time you streaked across that polo field at James Golding's wedding?'

Rob's look threatened to cut him off at the knees.

'Or the time you drank that red wine and spewed all over your girlfriend's mother's priceless Persian rug?'

God, what he wouldn't do to be able to kick Patrick out of the vehicle. Had he always been this much of a pain and he just hadn't noticed?

Patrick's mobile rang in his pocket.

'Saved by the bell… Hey—hi, Dad. I'm having a freaky moment because your favourite nephew is taking me to meet a *girl*!'

Patrick listened for a moment, and then Rob sucked in his breath when all the colour drained from his cousin's face.

'What?' Rob demanded. 'What is it?'

'You need to get me to the airport. Now.'

* * *

After she'd received a text from Rob saying that he couldn't make dinner at Saints, Willa spent the evening trawling the net, looking for job opportunities in accounting and business and wishing plagues of blood-sucking locusts on every advertiser who used the words 'experienced' or 'proven track record'. And there were a lot.

Willa banged her head against the sleek desk in the study-cum-library, empty of books but full of light, and cursed the prickling in her eyes that suggested tears were a hair's breadth away.

She was starting to get desperate, and was actually thinking that she should call the one person who could land her a job with just a call or two. Wayne-the-Pain had connections on Mars, and any of the many accountancy firms he'd had dealings with over the years would find a position for anyone he suggested.

There was just a tiny problem with that scenario—actually, two problems. The first was that she'd rather boil her head in tar than ask him for anything, and the second was that he thought she had the intelligence of a tree stump.

Oh, and there was also a number three problem. The Pain thought that she had bought her degree with *his* money.

So, to summarise, calling her ex was not an option.

Willa banged her forehead on the desk again and just stayed there, her cheek lying on the cool surface.

'You look like I feel,' Rob said.

Willa lifted her head and looked at him, tall and strong, standing in the doorway to her study, hands gripping the doorframe above his head, biceps bulging. He often stood like that, and Willa knew that he had no idea how sexy he looked.

'Your front door was unlocked again.'

She had to start being more conscientious about that.

She was no longer living in an apartment with a private lift and a twenty-four-seven doorman.

Rob walked over to her, briefly covered her lips in a kiss hello, and perched his butt on the edge of the desk. He ran his hand through his hair and looked out of the window. He looked tired again, she thought, and worried. The fine lines around his eyes were deeper and his lips were compressed in a tight line.

Willa placed her feet on the desk and nudged his thigh with her big toe. 'Are you okay? You look played out.'

Rob picked up a glass paperweight and tossed it from hand to hand. 'I just had to take my cousin to the airport. His wife and little girl—my goddaughter—have had a car accident and both are in hospital.'

Willa dropped her feet with a bang. 'Oh, no! Are they okay?'

'Kiley, their baby girl, is in for observation, and Heather has a broken collarbone and a couple of broken ribs. Lacerations. Obviously Patrick needs to be with them, so we raced to the airport and got him on the first flight out. I thought about going with him but he said that it's not necessary; we have lots of family in Jo'burg to help out and there's so much to do here.'

'I'm sorry, Rob. I'm sure they'll both be fine.'

A muscle ticked in Rob's jaw as he stared out of the huge windows that overlooked the pool.

'I know…and I really feel crap and selfish for thinking this…but…' he dropped an F-bomb '…this couldn't have happened at a worse time. I need Patrick *here*. He was wading through and more importantly understanding the minefield we're negotiating to get these companies set up. I thought that the officials back home liked red tape, but your government is giving them a damn good run for their money. It should be simple. I want to open a business, pay your exorbitant taxes, employ some of your people and make some money. Why does it have to be so frigging difficult?'

'It's not—'

Rob spoke over her. 'Patrick won't be back for weeks, and now I have to find someone I can work with in a city where I know no one. I suppose asking for someone I can trust would be like asking for moon dust.'

'You know *me*. And you can trust me.'

'I don't trust anyone—and, sorry, but I don't think you can help me out with this particular problem,' Rob muttered, jumping off the desk to pace the area in front of the windows.

Willa glared at his back. 'And what does that mean?'

Rob ignored her question, his mind millions of miles away. 'Didn't you say that your ex is a hotshot businessman? Who does *he* use?'

'Excuse me?' Willa managed to get the words out as a fine red mist descended in front of her eyes.

'Who are his accountants? Come on—surely you know that much?' Rob retorted, impatient.

Willa climbed to her feet, pulling in deep breaths as she struggled to hold on to her bubbling temper. 'Are you *kidding* me?' she gasped, feeling side-winded by his lack of sensitivity. And, worse, hurt. Dammit, she'd promised herself that she wasn't going to allow men to hurt her any more! 'You son of a bitch!'

'What?' Rob frowned. 'What's your problem?'

'You! *You're* my friggin' problem! Asking me about Wayne's connections! In between shagging me, did you even hear anything I said about what I studied? What I'd like to do?' Willa shouted. Oh, wow, another part of her wondered, when had she last shouted? Lost her temper?

That would be, like, *never*.

'You studied accounting… What's that got to do with me?' Rob asked.

Willa felt like launching the glass paperweight at his head. She waited until he'd connected the dots and then he looked puzzled.

'Oh, come on, Willa—you don't *really* think that you can take Patrick's place?'

Willa slapped her hands on her hips. 'Why the hell not?'

'Because he's got fifteen years of business experience, has been a CA for ten, and I trust him with my life and—more importantly—with our business!' Rob snarled. 'Are you seriously suggesting that you can do his job? You don't even have any experience in bookkeeping!'

'I'd like someone to give me some damn credit!'

Willa bent down and yanked open the deep drawer of the desk. She pulled a folder out of the concealed filing cabinet. Slapping it onto the desk, she flipped it open and removed some pages. Stomping over to him, she smacked the papers against his chest.

'I have a Master's degree in commerce. I graduated summa cum laude. In case you've forgotten what that means, that's the highest honours. I majored in accountancy and business law. I am *not* a freaking bookkeeper!'

Willa's chest heaved and bright splotches appeared on her throat and neck. 'You insensitive, insulting...*clod*! Now, take a walk back through my unlocked door and keep walking! Not even your excellent skills in the sack are worth putting up with this amount of BS and such lack of respect from you!'

Rob looked at the certificates in his hand and closed his eyes. 'Dammit, Willa, I'm—'

If she couldn't have his respect then she definitely didn't need his apologies.

Holding up her hand to stop him talking, she shook her head. 'Stop. Just get out.'

Rob looked stubborn. 'I'm not leaving.'

Willa narrowed her eyes; he was either six one or six

two of solid muscle, and she'd need a crane or the police to shift him if he didn't want to move. She had no intention of using either. 'Fine. Then I'll leave.'

Striding towards the door, she blinked back tears as she looked at the ceiling. *One teeny, tiny break here, universe? Any chance of that, huh?*

Hours and too many tears later, Willa walked into her kitchen and closed her eyes when she saw Rob at the stove, a pink apron tied around his hips. It took a man very secure in his masculinity to pull that look off—then again, she knew that Rob had no issues with his masculinity. Neither did she. But as cute as he looked—and he did look cute in his black basketball shorts, red T-shirt and the frothy pink apron—she was still not happy that he was in her space, in her house, in her life…

Okay, that was a lie; maybe she was a little happy. He might be a stupid, insensitive male, but he was still pretty. And it looked as if he was making…was that pot roast? Striding over to the oven, she yanked open the door, nearly smacking Rob in the shoulder as she did so. Damn—missed. She wished she'd had a better aim or he'd had slower reactions.

Pot roast, roasted vegetables, peas…all her favourites. She was instantly catapulted back to helping her mum make Sunday lunch.

Willa bit her lip as Rob gently shut the door, and she didn't resist when he linked his arms around her stomach and pulled her back into his chest.

'How did you know?' she whispered.

'Know what?'

'To make me that…it's my favourite meal ever.'

Rob turned her around and pushed her fringe out of her eyes. 'I didn't. I was just hungry and I was looking for something to do while you got over your—'

Willa glared at him and he was smart enough to snap off his words.

'While I waited for you.' Rob rubbed her cheekbone with his thumb as his hand clasped the side of her face. 'I'm sorry that I hurt you. That what I said came across as me insulting your intelligence.'

Willa sighed. 'You *did* insult my intelligence,' she pointed out.

'I questioned your experience, Willa, not your degree— which is impressive, by the way.'

Willa stepped away from him and held her hand against her forehead. 'It doesn't make the sting go away, Rob! Tell me, please, how am I supposed to prove to anyone—you— that I can do the job if no one—you—will allow me to prove that I can?'

Rob walked away from her and went to the fridge, pulling out a bottle of beer. 'Want a glass of wine?' he asked.

Willa glanced at the wall clock, surprised to see that it was past nine—way past wine o'clock. And, dammit, she needed a little pick-me-up. 'Hell, yes.'

Rob pulled a bottle of wine from the fridge and took the glass that Willa handed him. So working for him was out of the question. She understood, intellectually, that she was too inexperienced for him to trust her with his precious company. Her business brain understood his reluctance, but the rest of her wanted to pound her fists against his chest and wail like a child, screaming that the world was a horrible, unfair place.

Nobody had ever said that life was fair, she reminded herself.

Rob took a long pull of his beer and Willa couldn't help noticing the masculine up and down movement of his throat, the width of his shoulders. His eyes were more blue than grey today. He met her gaze and passion, hot and wild, arced between them. Instead of moving towards her,

as she'd expected him to, he lowered the bottle and slid onto
a bucket-shaped stool at the granite counter.

'I went to every single bank I could to raise the money
to buy into my uncle's gym. Every single bank manager I
met—all of them fat and unfit, I might add—told me that I
had no collateral. I didn't. And, worse, I had no experience.'

Willa leaned her arms on the counter, interested despite
her irritation. 'So how did you raise the money?'

Rob peeled the sticker off his beer bottle. 'My mum
cashed in her pension fund. I nearly had a heart attack
when she gave me the cheque. I was so angry with her;
my father had left her some money—but her pension fund?
Craziness.'

'Did you refuse to take it?'

'I did. Until she told me that I either took it or she was
going to go on a world cruise and pick up as many dis-
reputable men as she could who would help her spend it.'

Willa smiled.

'She would've too; she's the most stubborn woman I've
ever met. Anyway, I bought the gym. Then Patrick and
I opened another one, and the old saying that it's easy to
get money out of the banks when you already have money
turned out to be true. I repaid my mum,' he added.

'Of course you did.' Of that she had no doubt. The man
was a clot, not a scummy conman.

'I'm trying to make a point here...'

He was? Willa had just thought they were having idle
conversation. 'Which is...?'

'No one would give *me* a chance either and I proved
them wrong. Maybe I should give you the same chance.'

It took a moment for the words to sink in, to make sense
in her jumbled brain, but when they did Willa felt the sweet
sensation of joy roll through her.

Telling herself not to get her hopes up, she lifted her eyes
to Rob. 'Please don't toy with me,' she pleaded with him.

'I'm not. But I'm also not risking my business on your inexperience. So I'll make you a deal.'

'What deal?'

'You start at the beginning—pretend that I'm a new investor. Make a list of the steps I need to take, detailing what you think I should I do, look out for. Back your opinions up with the relevant legislation… If you come up with a plan of action that is the same as Patrick's we're in business and I'll hire you as my Australian accountant.'

Willa looked at him in astonishment. 'Are you being serious?'

Rob's mouth twitched at the corners. 'Not up for the challenge?'

'Of course I am!' Willa swallowed her squeal. 'How long do I have?'

Rob cocked his head. 'Two days?'

'You're on.'

Willa slid off her chair and walked past Rob, who grabbed her by the seat of her pants and pulled her back.

'Where do you think you're going?'

Willa looked at him, surprised. 'To work. I've got a stack of research to do.'

Rob spun her around and pulled her between his open thighs. 'Your pot roast will be ready in fifteen minutes.'

Willa looked longingly towards the oven. 'Okay, I'll work after supper.'

'After supper you *will* work—and it will have nothing to do with corporations and trusts and Inland Revenue,' Rob said against her mouth.

Willa placed her hands on his thighs and felt the long muscles under her hands contract.

'Tomorrow will be soon enough for you to get all nerdy and geeky and accountanty,' Rob told her.

'I *am* geeky and nerdy,' Willa told him. 'I even have those big black nerd glasses.'

'I *love* those. You'll have to wear them for me—naked.'

Willa pulled her head back and laughed up into his eyes. 'Give me the job and I will.'

CHAPTER SIX

TWO DAYS LATER, after a long, long day interviewing personal trainers and admin staff, Rob was grateful to be off the clock—or as much off the clock as you could be when you owned your own business. It was a stunningly beautiful summer's evening, still hot, and it was way past time for a beer and some downtime.

He was at Willa's house—palace, mansion, whatever—and inside was a woman, cold beer and fantastic sex.

He'd certainly landed with his bread butter side up woman-wise, he thought as he dropped his keys and mobile into the ceramic bowl on the hall table. Willa was fun and uncomplicated, easy to be around, and—perhaps surprisingly—she enjoyed sex as much as he did. In his arms, naked, she became a sensual, demanding woman who wasn't afraid to tell him what she wanted and how she wanted it.

Yes, the gods of a good time were sure smiling on him. If they could bring the gods of getting his business up and running to the party he'd be eternally grateful.

'Oh, good, you're here. *Finally.*'

Rob turned, looked at the creature who'd spoken to him, and blinked. Tailored black pants, stark white shirt, thick mahogany hair pulled back into a severe twist. Willa nearly always greeted him in shorts and a tank over a bikini—why was she dressed up like corporate mannequin?

'Hi. You look…businesslike.'

'That's the point. But before we get to that, how is your cousin's wife, his daughter? I've been thinking about them.'

Rob felt touched that she'd thought to ask. 'They are both at home, recovering. Patrick has started to breathe again.'

'I'm so glad,' Willa replied. 'So...can I see you in my study?'

Rob frowned at her crisp voice and briefly wondered—okay, hoped—that this was the start of a role-playing game in which he ended up taking her from behind as she leaned over her desk, that delicious butt in the air.

'Can I get a beer first?' he asked, veering off towards the kitchen.

'Afterwards,' Willa insisted, taking his hand and pulling him down the passage.

Rob allowed her to push him into the chair on the other side of her desk and waited from her to straddle him—because if he couldn't get a beer then he wanted sex. Then a beer, then a swim, then more sex and possibly dinner. Then more sex—if he hadn't passed out or dropped dead by then...

Rob jumped as Willa tossed a thick bound document into his lap. Frowning, he flipped it over. 'What's this?'

'You gave me two days to gather information for you on setting up your company in Australia.' Willa sat down in the chair behind her desk and looked at him. 'That is what I came up with.'

Rob looked down at the professional-looking document in his hand and back to Willa, who was looking nervous and hopeful and...petrified.

Rob ran his hand over his jaw. *You're treading on some-one's dreams here, Hanson, do not open your big mouth and shatter her illusions. For once in your life be gentle. Or at least tactful.*

When Willa hadn't mentioned his little test again he'd almost presumed that she'd thought it too much of a has-sle. He'd sort of thought that she liked the *idea* of working more than she was actually prepared to work...

Convinced that she wouldn't actually take him up on his offer, he'd put out some feelers to the bigger accounting and finance companies in Sydney, in case she didn't have the smarts, or the courage, to do the job.

He start to flip pages and whistled at the detail she'd gone into. He'd underestimated her, he quickly realised, and badly. There were SWOT analyses, alternative suggestions on how to set up his company legally, and a checklist of all the paperwork that needed to be submitted to the relevant authorities to become compliant. She'd gone above and beyond and— *Holy hell!* A paragraph caught his eye. He'd never thought of that. Neither, it seemed, had Patrick.

And if they set the company up as she suggested they would avoid some of the nasty and complicated regulations that governed foreign-owned entities.

'When I said that I wanted a list of what needed to be done I expected a page or two—not a doctoral thesis.'

Willa shrugged. 'What can I say? I'm an over-achiever and it was fun…putting my brain and training to work.'

Rob tapped the folder and held her eyes. 'Good job, Willa. I'm seriously impressed.'

Willa sucked in her breath, hope shining from her eyes. 'Impressed enough to give me the job?'

Rob, hoping that he wasn't making a huge mistake, slowly nodded. 'Yeah. I'm handing the paperwork over to you.'

Willa shot up so fast that she skidded backwards over the polished wooden floor and did a crazy dance on the spot. 'Yes! Yes, yes, yes, *yes*!'

Rob grinned and watched the years roll off her as she went a little silly. He sat back in his chair and placed his ankle on his knee, watching her twirl around. What a waste of her brain these last eight years had been, he thought. Her solution to his business's greatest stumbling block was simple and clear-thinking and neither he nor Patrick had even come close to thinking of it.

Hell, for that alone he would have hired her. But, although he'd only skimmed through the document, there was also a wad of information in there that he could use, as well as steps towards what they needed to achieve.

Whoomph!

Rob tensed as a bundle of warm, fragrant flesh fell into his lap and a feminine mouth started placing kisses all over his face.

'Gerrrooofffff!' he muttered, gently placing his hand on her face and pushing her away. 'Stop doing that.'

Willa launched herself at him again, kissing his temple. 'I absolutely won't. Thank you—' kiss '—thank you—' kiss '—thank you.'

'Okay, enough already.' Rob leaned back out of her reach.

Willa, her legs straddling his thighs, grinned at him. 'Why? Shouldn't I be kissing my boss like that?'

She looked horrified, and Rob knew exactly what she was thinking.

'Oh, hell...maybe I shouldn't be kissing you at all!'

Rob chuckled. 'Don't be silly, Willa. Kiss me—just not like a sloppy puppy.'

Willa remained serious and he sighed. She was going to complicate this, he could just tell.

'Maybe we shouldn't if we're going to work together,' she said, gnawing on her bottom lip.

'Stop that.' He tapped her lip with his finger. 'That's my job.' He sighed. 'Don't worry, gorgeous. You're going to work for me and we're going to keep sleeping together until my company is up and running and I go back to South Africa. Work is work and everything else is fun...is that clear?'

Willa pursed her lips. 'S'pose.'

Rob flashed her a grin as his hands drifted over her stomach and then up to cup her breasts, his thumbs easily finding her nipples and rubbing them into hard points.

'You have the prettiest body,' he muttered, going to work on the buttons of her shirt, cursing as his big fingers battled to pull them through their tiny slits. 'To hell with this!'

He ripped her shirt open. Willa just looked at him, and then down at her transparent bra.

'I didn't like the shirt, but don't you *dare* rip this bra....' Willa retorted—and then stopped speaking as he sucked her, fabric and all, into his mouth.

Willa responded to the rasp of the fabric against her ultra-sensitised nipples and moaned, grinding into his hard erection, which was perfectly placed to give her the maximum pleasure.

Rob, not in the mood to wait, or to take orders from her, flashed her a naughty grin and with one twist detached a see-through triangle from its strap.

Willa's mouth dropped open as the material fluttered down. 'Dammit, Rob, I told you not to rip it! Now you're not getting the glasses!'

No sexy nerd glasses? *Oh, damn.* 'Couldn't you have told me that earlier?' he complained, his hand coming up to rest on her bare breast. 'Please? Pretty please?'

Willa tried to look annoyed—which she did well, considering that she was rotating her hips and sliding against the pipe in his pants.

'No.'

Rob grabbed her hips and lifted her off him, easily holding her in the air. 'Then you don't get to do *that*.'

Willa thought for a moment and then wriggled off his lap. Standing with her back to him, in between him and the desk, she stripped off her shirt and the broken bra and quickly shimmied her pants over her hips. Keeping her strappy sandals on, she stretched as Rob played with the beaded T of her G-string. His heart picked up pace as he traced the cleft of her buttocks, touching the skin under the gossamer band of her thong.

'These make men stupid,' he muttered, placing an open-mouthed kiss on one of the two dents above her butt cheeks.

Pulling the clip that kept her hair off her neck, Willa shook her head and her hair tumbled down, heavy and thick against her back. Leaning across the desk, she picked up her heavy glasses and slipped them onto her nose.

'Let's see you, numbers nerd,' Rob ordered and, his hands on her hips, spun her around.

She gripped the desk with her hands as she leaned back, her back arched provocatively, her hips tilted and her eyes lowered in passion.

Damn, she had no idea how sexy she was, Rob thought, looking up into those eyes that echoed the waters of the bay. He'd never quite understood the expression 'drowning in her eyes', and had thought that it was over-used by poets and posers until this very minute. They were deep and mysterious and held a million secrets…

She was such a contradiction, Rob thought, leaning forward and taking a moment to slow his heart down by resting his forehead on her fragrant stomach. Amazingly, shockingly bright, a little naïve, a lot innocent. Stronger than she realised and tougher than she gave herself credit for. In another life, if he was another guy, he'd be finding a way to make her his…

But he couldn't give her anything more—*be* her anything more. Apart from the fact that his time here was limited, relationships of any depth or length required trust—and that wasn't something he could do. *Ever.*

Still, this woman was the first in a very long time—okay, in for ever—who had made him even consider that possibility. And that was why he had to be doubly careful around her… They were sleeping together and now working together. The lines were getting blurred very fast indeed.

Slow it down, moron. Seriously. Because someone is going to get certain parts of his anatomy put through a grinder. His heart and his balls ran for cover at the thought…

All he had—all he *could* have—was right now, and he could suck the life out of every moment with this woman. And he intended to, he thought as he slowly stood up.

Instead of kissing her upturned mouth Rob dropped feather-light kisses on her collarbone, nibbled her neck, and sucked on that sweet spot between her neck and ear. Willa tipped her head to allow him better access and picked up his hand and placed it on her breast. To tease her he just held her in his palm, but she growled her disapproval and pushed her breast into his hand.

'I need you to touch me.'

Rob laughed lightly. 'Getting there,' he replied.

This was his fantasy and he wouldn't be rushed. So he teased and tormented; tasting the skin on the inside of her elbow, the top of her hip. He nuzzled the inside of her thighs, explored her knees, and tangled his tongue in the fine three-strand chain around her slim ankle. He feasted. And when he thought Willa couldn't stand another minute more he started the process all over again.

When he finally pulled her thong to one side and found her sweet spot with his tongue she orgasmed instantly, and he slid two fingers into her and nuzzled her to another high. As pliant as a doll, she let him spin her around. He laid her across the desk and unzipped his cargo shorts. Taking the condom from his back pocket—he'd taken to carrying one around for situations just like these—he rolled it on and, spreading her legs, slid into her wet wild warmth and rotated his hips. So hot, so deep, so *Willa*.

Happy to delay his pleasure, he lay across her back,

content to stay sheathed in her, running his hands up and down her sides before sliding them around to her front and stroking her nipples with his thumbs.

Willa, being Willa, slowly stirred, and he felt her push back against him, recognised the tension in her body that he'd come to know so well. She was up for another orgasm and he would give her one—slow and hot...

Except it didn't happen the way he'd intended. She pushed back and he hit her G-spot—and suddenly she was demanding more, and he was pumping, and if he had to stop he would just die...

He heard Willa scream and felt her clench around him and another burst of pure energy pulsed through him.

Yeah, Rob thought as he locked his knees to keep himself from collapsing. It wasn't love, or for ever, but it was still damned amazing.

He could live with that.

'Need coffee,' Willa muttered, her face in Rob's shoulder.

This was fair, because something of his was still buried in her as well.

Rob patted her butt. 'It's your turn. I made it yesterday morning.'

'You make better coffee.'

'This is true, but it's still your turn.' Rob pulled his head away to look into her face. *'Ack...*don't we sound domesticated?'

They did—and she liked it, Willa thought. Better watch that or else she would get accustomed to waking up to Rob and going to sleep with Rob as well as sleeping with Rob.

Willa rolled off him and sighed, pushing her tangled hair out of her face. Who was she trying to fool...? She was already getting used to all of the above. *And* his coffee.

No doing anything stupid, here, Willa—like falling for

him in any way, shape or form. She was not going to be moronic about this…

Rob walked to the en-suite bathroom. She heard the toilet flush and a burst of water suggesting that he was brushing his teeth or washing his hands. Probably both. Willa rolled onto her stomach, turned her head to the window and looked out onto the bay. It was a gorgeous summer's day, and if she and Rob weren't up to their ears in work she'd suggest that they take a canoe and snorkelling equipment into the reserve and have a picnic.

It was Saturday, after all.

'Guess I'm making coffee.'

She flicked her eyes to the free-standing mirror to her right and saw that Rob had pulled on a pair of shorts and was looking fit and hot and—more importantly—awake.

'How do you *do* that?' she grumbled.

Rob walked around the bed and sat on the edge, placing his hand on her hip. 'Do what?'

'Look all chipper and raring to go? Especially after sex?'

'Sex energises me.' The corners of that amazing mouth—so talented—tipped up. 'I've been feeling very energetic lately.'

Willa smiled. They had been going at it like muskrats—or whatever animal it was that bonked like crazy.

'And laziness, moving slow, is a habit,' Rob added. 'I've noticed that people who don't have to get moving quickly—to get to work on time, to make appointments—are perpetually lazy. *And* late.'

That was true; Willa admitted reluctantly. She had little sense of time and was nearly always late to everything.

Rob's expression turned serious. 'That's something that you're going to have to work on, Willa. I hate people not being punctual and I hate laziness.'

Willa slowly sat up and tried to ignore the flash of hurt annoyance coursing through her. 'I'm not lazy…'

Rob just looked at her, his face implacable. 'Yeah, you are. And why shouldn't you be? You spent the last eight years being told to look pretty, to do nothing, be ornamental. It doesn't work for me.'

Willa said the first thing that came to mind. 'Good thing you're not sticking around, then.'

Rob's hand gripped her thigh and squeezed. 'Except that you are now working for me...and I expect my pound of flesh. Work-wise. That's a solid eight, maybe a ten, sometimes twelve-hour day.'

Willa blinked at him. 'God!'

'I need to know that you can work until the job is done... If you don't think you can then maybe you should say so now, before we go any further. No hard feelings. I'll just find someone else.'

Like hell he would. Willa felt something swell in her throat and thought it might be pride—or something close to it. He was *not* going to dismiss her, think less of her, just because she'd sat on her backside for eight years...

'I wasn't given a choice to do anything else,' she protested.

Rob shook his head. 'I don't accept that, Willa. You *always* have a choice. The choices might be hard, but there is always something to choose between.'

'You don't know what it was like, living with him.'

'Probably not.' Rob agreed. 'But I believe that we live with the consequences of the choices we make. For years you lived with the consequences of staying with your husband and that was your choice. Now you're living with the consequences of divorcing him—which...' he looked around '...don't seem to be that bad. But none of that has anything to do with me...'

'Exactly,' Willa murmured, vastly irritated.

'But what *does* concern me is your work ethic and whether you can pull your weight with me. I run fast and

I run hard and I expect you to keep up. You don't—you're fired.'

Willa closed her eyes at his brutal statement. His bald honestly had the ability to scald skin, she thought. Yet, that being said, it was still a sweet pain. For the first time in her life she knew exactly where she stood, what was expected of her. And nobody was going to give her a head start because of who she was connected to. For the first time ever she was going to sink or swim and she was in control.

It was her choice…

She lifted her chin and looked Rob straight in the eye. 'I choose to work my ass off.'

'Good. I expect nothing less.'

Nobody had ever been this forthright with her, this honest. She'd always been handled with kid gloves and it was both enthralling and annoying, to be treated so… She wanted to say so carelessly, but that wasn't fair to Rob. He wasn't a careless man but he *was* demanding. He had a high set of expectations and he expected her to reach them. She didn't intend to let him down.

More importantly, she didn't intend to let herself down.

'Let's go out tonight,' Rob suggested, changing the subject adroitly.

Her lover was back and her boss had—temporarily, she was sure—left the building. She couldn't keep up with who she was dealing with and she didn't like it. And if she didn't put her foot down now… What was Kate's favourite saying? *You teach people how to treat you…*

'This isn't going to work for me,' she stated firmly.

'What? Having some dinner? Seeing a show?'

'That too, but no… You flipping between boss and lover.' Willa pushed her hair back and waved at the bed. 'I declare this a no work zone.'

'I've lost you. Explain.'

Willa made herself meet his eyes. 'You can't segue from

talking about sex and how it energises you into making a comment about my work habits and what you expect. And then switch back to lover mode and talk about where we should eat dinner. That's not fair. When you're in my bed, when we're naked, you don't get to say things like that.'

Willa held her breath as she saw the emotions run through Rob's eyes. She was starting to be able to read his eyes, she thought. Irritation, thoughtfulness…embarrassment?

Rob rubbed the back of his neck before reaching over to cup her face. 'You're right.'

You're right? That was it? No comeback? No long speech asking how she could possibly think that, that he had a right to say what he—?

'I'm sorry.'

He was *apologising*? Holy smokes! Seriously?

'That's okay.' Willa managed to get the words out despite her astonishment. A big, alpha man who wasn't afraid to admit he was wrong? She hadn't thought they made that type of man any more.

'So—new rule. We only talk business in the study… Everywhere else, especially the bedroom, is off bounds for work and business,' Rob reiterated. 'Okay, sorted. Now, about dinner…'

Willa took a moment to get with the programme, still amazed at how easily the issue had been resolved. She pulled a face. 'I would love to, but I can't. I have a fiftieth birthday party to attend.'

'I thought you said that you don't have any friends in Sydney?'

'Well, I don't…not really. Except for Misha and Vern. It's his fiftieth birthday party and they've begged me to come. I'm absolutely dreading it.'

'Because the douche will be there?' Rob guessed.

'Yeah.'

'So don't go. Life is too short to do things you don't want to. Blow it off. Let's go have some fun instead.'

She wanted to, but she couldn't. Misha and Vern had been her biggest allies and staunchest defenders when she'd been married to Wayne. They were one of the most influential and nice couples in that elevated social strata.

Unlike the wives and girlfriends of Wayne's friends and business cronies, Willa hadn't had children or a career, and she'd hovered on the outside of their group, rebuffed one too many times to make much of an effort to be included. The husbands had been a different story: to them she'd been fair game. She'd been groped, hassled and propositioned, and whenever she'd complained to Wayne he'd accused her of looking for attention.

Walking back into that den of vipers would stir up gossip, and she would have to endure not only seeing Wayne again but the nasty asides, the up and down looks, the sotto voce comments behind manicured hands.

'Misha and Vern were always nice to me—my social haven, if you will. They were always happy to include me in their conversations, at their table, welcoming my opinions. Attending Vern's birthday bash is my way of showing my appreciation,' Willa stated.

'Do you want me to come with you?'

Willa stared at Rob's hand on her thigh, broad and masculine. Of *course* she wanted him to come with her—what could be better than walking in with a super-sexy new man on her arm?—but she refused to ask him. She could—*would*—do this on her own if she had to. She wasn't the same person she'd been then; she was stronger, happier, confident.

'What's the dress code, where is the party, and what time do we have to be there?' Rob asked.

Willa imagined punching the air and doing a crazy happy dance but she kept her face straight. 'Black tie, on a yacht in Campbell's Cove, at eight. Thank you for offering to escort me.'

'Like those expressive eyes of yours weren't begging me to,' Rob scoffed, leaning forward to brush his mouth across hers briefly.

'It'll be staid and stuffy and Wayne will most definitely make an appearance.'

Rob raised an eyebrow. 'Are you trying to talk me out of going with you?'

'I just want to make sure you know what you're *volunteering* for. You don't have to come if you really don't want to.' Willa lifted her chin. 'I can and will go on my own. I'll be absolutely fine.'

'Sure you will—but you'll be a hell of a lot better with me,' Rob shot back, and shoved his hand through his messy hair.

Yeah. No arguing with that.

'Look, Willa, I'm not totally insensitive or emotionally stunted. I can see that you'd rather walk on broken glass than go, but I admire your sense of loyalty—and, trust me, I'm as surprised by my offer to go with you as anyone. It's not something I'd usually waste my time on, but you look like you could do with some support and it looks like I'm it. Why do I suspect that too few people have really been there for you when you needed them to be?'

Willa blinked her tears away and licked her lips. Wasn't that the truth? She knew that her father and brother loved her, but her father wanted her to have a perfect life, to be protected, and she and Luke had never been close. She'd allowed her friendships with the people she met at the Weeping Reef resort to fade away when she'd stepped into Wayne's world—only to find out that his world was a hard place and that her husband, so charming and charismatic on holiday, was the King of Cold and Cruel.

God, didn't she sound melodramatic? But it was only

now that she was standing in the sun she realised how frozen she'd been. She knew that she was being irrational, but she felt that the party tonight had the ability to flash-freeze her again.

Rob lifted her chin in order to make her look at him. She didn't know that her eyes were large and miserable and soul-deep scared.

'You don't have to go,' he reiterated.

'I do. For Misha and Vern and for my pride.'

'Okay, then. I'll be with you every minute, and to get to you Wayne will have to go through me,' Rob promised her. 'Trust me, I'm more than a match for him.'

Willa looped her arms around his neck and placed her face on his shoulder. 'Thanks.'

Rob's hand brushed over her hair, down her spine. 'I've got your back, Willa.'

CHAPTER SEVEN

LATER THAT MORNING Willa left Rob to work out in her gym and headed to Surry Hills for lunch with her girls. She now had 'girls', she thought as she spotted Kate's bright red head at the back of the restaurant. Kate and Amy and…Jessica.

Jessica—who seemed to collect people like some women collected shoes. And that was okay, Willa thought. It wasn't as if she had so many friends that she could refuse the offer of friendship from anyone.

Willa, dressed in a bright pink halterneck dress and peony-pink flip-flops, hair up in a tail, grinned at her friends as she slipped into the empty fourth chair.

'Dear God,' Amy murmured. 'You're *so* getting lucky.'

Willa grinned. 'I so am…' Turning to the waiter, she placed her order for a virgin mojito.

'What's the point?' Amy cried.

'The last time I drank with you I woke up to a stranger in my bed and a house full of guests,' Willa explained.

'The stranger is still there, bonking your brains out, and you told me that it was a fabby party,' Kate replied crisply. 'Add the booze,' she told the waitress.

When Kate used that tone of voice nobody argued.

The waitress snapped her chewing gum and grinned. 'Sure. Something to eat?'

'Later, honey, thanks—just bring the drinks, please,' Kate said, and waved her away. She leaned back in her chair and sent Willa a thoughtful look. 'This isn't just about sex…something else has happened.'

Kate, after spending so many hours with Willa hammering out her divorce, had become something of a big sister, and probably knew Willa better than any person alive. She'd held her hand, mopped up her tears and—metaphorically—slapped some sense into her. Kate had ripped the rose-coloured glasses off her eyes and had made her grow up, and for that Willa would be eternally grateful.

Willa's eyes sparkled with delight and she wiggled in her seat like a puppy waiting for a milk bone. 'I've got a job.'

Amy whooped her delight and Kate, far more controlled, squeezed her hand.

Leaning across the table, Jessica high-fived her. 'That's fantastic, Willa. I'm so happy for you…'

'With who? When do you start?' Kate demanded.

'Rob's accountant had to fly back home for a family emergency and Rob said that I can take over.' Willa's words bubbled like champagne. 'And there's so much to do… He's just handed everything financial over to—'

Willa looked around the suddenly sombre faces and frowned. It was as if someone had just tossed an icy bucket of water over her friends and they were less than amused.

'What's the matter?'

Amy looked at Kate, who lifted her eyebrows in response. Neither of them said anything.

'Okay, you guys are starting to scare me,' Willa said, her hand on her heart. 'Two seconds ago you were happy for me and now you're exchanging *what-the-hell-has-she-done?* looks across the table.'

Amy took a sip of her wine and waited until their perky waitress had placed Willa's mojito in front of her and left before speaking again. 'When you said you had a job we thought you meant a real job.'

Excuse me? What? 'A real job? Sorting out Rob's company finances is a hell of a job, thank you very much.'

'It's a job with someone you're sleeping with,' Amy murmured.

'Is he actually paying you?' Jessica asked baldly before Willa could respond.

'Uh…' They hadn't actually discussed that. She hoped so, but frankly she'd work for free to get the experience she so desperately needed.

Kate rolled her eyes. 'Hell, Willa, have I taught you nothing about protecting yourself?'

Willa frowned, not really understanding how she'd coloured outside the lines. 'I've lost you.'

'Rob is sleeping with you and you're now working for him as well? If you tell me that you're cooking for him and doing his laundry I will slap you,' Amy told her. 'Look, don't get me wrong, I like Rob—but he's not a keeper. What are *you* getting out of what looks to be a very one-sided relationship?'

'Good sex?' Willa quipped. 'Oh, lighten up, all of you, I'm not a complete idiot! Firstly, it's not a relationship… we're having fun together as long as he is in the country. There are no expectations on either side.'

Under the table, Willa crossed her legs.

'As for me working for him—even if it wasn't the most challenging work I've done…ever!…I'd be a fool not to do it because I am out of options. When Rob goes I can put working for him on my CV—show that I have the experience people keep telling me I need to get a decent job. That's golden, girls. I am not doing this to make him happy. I'm doing it because it benefits *me*.'

Amy still didn't look convinced. 'You're not the type to keep it light and fluffy, Wills.'

'Trust me—I've learnt. I'm not the naïve innocent you used to know, Amy. I'm a bit wiser, I hope. I'm not stupid enough to hand over my heart again for someone to stomp on it. Besides, Rob would tell me to put it away and stop looking for hearts and flowers.'

'Good girl.' Kate nodded. 'As long as you're thinking with your head and not your va-jay-jay.'

'God, Kate,' Jessica muttered, after choking on her sip of wine. 'What an expression!'

'My grandma heard it on TV and now she uses it all the time. She says it's only fair that if men think with their penises then woman think with their…you know. Good for goose and gander and all that,' Kate explained.

'Your grandma sounds like a hoot,' Willa said, glad to have the spotlight off her.

'She and my mother were the original bra-burner and hippy chick. They constantly give me stick because I'm not fighting for the cause…'

'You're a brilliant family lawyer,' Willa protested.

'That I am,' Kate agreed. 'And a better divorce lawyer.'

Divorce—nearly there. The Pain…the party… Willa remembered where she had to be tonight and winced.

'You're pulling a face,' Kate muttered. 'Why are you pulling a face? What's happened? What's the matter?'

'Geez, take a tranq, Kate,' Willa told her. 'It's just that I have to attend a party tonight and Wayne-the-Pain will be there. I *so* don't want to go.'

'So don't go,' Jessica said, looking at the menu.

'That's what Rob said.' She wished she could see the world in black and white, as they seemed to, but for some reason her world held every shade of grey.

'You said that you've broken ties with Wayne's group. Why this function?' Amy asked. 'And, more importantly, should I have a beef or chicken burrito?'

Willa waited while her friends placed their food orders before explaining why she felt she had to attend, stirring her untouched mojito with her finger. 'I said I'd go, Kate. I know that you didn't want me to have any contact with Wayne, but—'

'Willa, that was when we were first negotiating your

divorce. The divorce papers are signed and lodged with the court now. They just need to go through the process. There's no going back from what we've negotiated. You could sleep together again and nothing would change.'

Willa mimed shoving a finger down her throat.

'So, are you going to go on your own or are you going to take Hot and Sexy with you?' Amy asked.

'He offered to come with me. Thank God. Because while I'm still dreading going, I'm dreading it marginally less.'

Kate placed her hand on her shoulder and squeezed. 'Wayne is not worth a minute of your time. Go tonight, be fabulous, act confident and look happy.'

'I *am* happy,' Willa stated, and the truth of that knowledge resonated deep inside her. And not only because she had a sexy man rumpling her sheets but because she felt like Willa—like herself. Not her father's princess, or Wayne's wife, or Luke's sister...just Willa. Young, strong, healthy, smart.

Willa.

Maybe she was starting to like who she was now. No, she *did* like who she was now...and wasn't that the best feeling in the world? Ever?

Dressed in a black suit, white shirt and a black tie—the closest he was ever going to get to a monkey suit—Rob stood in the kitchen and waited for Willa to come downstairs, a glass of red wine in his hands.

Dickied up and looking fly was not the way he wanted to spend his Saturday night...and normally it would take a gun to his head to get him to do something he didn't want to do... Yet here he was, prepared to play Willa's protector, her knight in a sharp black suit.

What was with that? He was nobody's white knight. He didn't want to play the role. He'd failed once in that role before. Which begged the question...why her? Why now?

Willa had come back from lunch sounding chipper, but as the afternoon had worn on and evening had approached she'd got quieter and more distant and he'd become…annoyed.

'Why are you going if you're dreading it so much?' he'd demanded, fed up with her silences. 'Why do you want to put yourself in that position? Just to say thank you to some people who were once nice to you? Send them a card, for God's sake!'

Willa's eyes had met his and they'd blazed bright. 'Obviously you've never felt less than unnoticed, lacking. But I have. And I am going to that party and I am going to hold my head up high and show them that I am *not* the wimpy wife they all thought I was. I do not want their last impression of me to be that quiet, insecure woman who was so easily dismissed. And I'll do it with or without you.'

His annoyance had faded after that as he'd realised how much guts it was going to take for her to walk into that room, filled with people who'd always dismissed her. This party was more than just making an appearance. It was her way to say goodbye to her old life, to walk away from those people and her waste-of-space ex with her head held high. She needed to go for her own pride and self-respect. He understood pride and self-respect and he appreciated Willa's courage.

His girl would be fine, Rob thought. Just the fact that she was doing this when it would be a lot easier not to told him that she was a stronger character than she realised.

"Respect, Willa."

Rob heard the click-clack of Willa's heels against the tiles and turned to look at her. The saliva dried up in his mouth. Dear God, she looked amazing. Like her eyes, her dress was silver shot through with green, clinging to her slim frame like a second skin. Thin cords held the dress up, crossed over her shoulders.

Rob lifted his finger and traced their outline. Willa obediently turned and his blood rushed out of his brain as he saw that the cords criss-crossed her smooth bare back to hold the fabric on either side of those back dimples he loved to kiss.

'How the hell did you get into that?' he asked.

'With difficulty,' Willa answered on a smile. 'Like it?'

'Hell, no—I love it and I can't wait to get you out of it,' Rob replied, taking a big sip of wine to lubricate his throat and to rehydrate his mouth. It didn't work. 'Want a drink?'

'Do we have time?' Willa asked, placing her silver clutch on the kitchen counter.

'Some. Besides, a dress like that deserves a late entrance. You look stunning.'

'Thank you. You don't look too shabby yourself.'

Willa took the half-glass of wine he held out and took a small sip.

'Why am I doing this, Rob?'

'You're taking back your self-respect,' Rob told her. 'That's always a fight worth fighting. *Always*, Willa. I wish I could...'

Respect myself again. Like myself again.

That one decision so long ago had changed everything.

Shut up, Hanson.

God! He'd never told anyone about his mother's disastrous second marriage, the part he'd played in it.

Willa cocked her head, her smoky eyes pinning him to the floor. 'You wish that you could...what?'

Rob rubbed the back of his neck, uncomfortable. 'Nothing—sorry. Thinking aloud.'

'I feel like you censor your words around me—that you start to tell me stuff and then you pull back.'

Rob couldn't lie to her. 'I do.'

'I'm a pretty good listener, Rob.'

'Honey, what's the point of listening if nothing can be

changed?' Rob replied, his tone low but resolute. 'Do you want some more wine?'

'If we don't get going I'm not going to go at all. I decided not to go to this party a hundred times today.' Willa tipped her head, staring at him with soul-searching eyes. 'I'd love to know one of your secrets, Rob, since you seem to be witnessing *all* of my little foibles, quirks and paranoias.'

Feeling like a butterfly pinned to a board, he shuffled his feet, torn between wanting to tell her about his past and wanting to run screaming into the night. In his head he opted for running and screaming.

He made a show of pushing back the cuff of his shirt to look at his watch. 'On second thoughts, leave the wine. I think we should get going.'

Willa slid off her chair and took the hand he held out. She picked up her clutch and hauled in a deep, deep breath.

Rob put his hand on her back. 'You okay?'

Willa managed a small smile. 'A hundred percent... If I tell you to turn the car around, just ignore me, okay?'

Rob, seeing the fine tremors that skittered through her body, pulled her in to his chest and wrapped his arms around her slight frame. Bending his head so that his mouth was on her ear, he spoke softly. 'You're not alone, Willa, not this time.'

Rob had attended his fair share of boring parties over the years—it was the price you paid when you did business with people who had money—but this one took 'boring' to new heights. The guests, around thirty in all, were either pompous, arrogant, annoying or all three at once, and no one tried to hide their curiosity about 'Willa's new man'.

'Willa's new man' couldn't give a rat's about what they thought of him, but he hated the up and down looks they gave Willa—as if any of the women here could hold a candle to her in the looks or brains department—and the insincere small talk they deigned to send her way.

Rob stood next to the bar on the enormous catamaran berthed in Campbell's Cove which, as Willa had told him, was one of the most picturesque super-yacht berths in the world. He could understand why. The marina was nestled between the Opera House and the Harbour Bridge and had outstanding views.

Sydney was a gorgeous city, Rob thought. He could see himself living here… He rubbed his eyes with his finger and thumb, wondering where that thought had come from. He loved his country, his home city, loved the energy and vibe of Jo'burg. Unlike many of his friends he'd never considered emigrating south. He was a born-and-bred African and he loved his South African life.

But, seriously, Oz wasn't that bad—and, he thought, looking at Willa's slim back as she spoke to their hosts, the girls weren't too shabby either. At least that one wasn't…

No one would believe that she'd spent the day as a bundle of nerves: she looked composed and dignified and super-hot.

'Willa *has* improved in the six months since we last saw her.'

Rob turned at the sound of a nasal voice at his elbow and met the calculating eyes of a brown-eyed brunette who'd spent far too much time in the sun—or, more likely, crisping herself on a sunbed. Eye-lift, boobs definitely fake and collagen lips. She was more plastic than cheap margarine.

And she was putting her bright red claws on his arm. *God*.

'So, where did our little Willa find *you*?' she drawled, empty martini glass in her hand. 'Or did she hire you?'

What. The. Hell.

'Excuse me?' he said, his voice low and containing a warning that she should be very, *very* careful.

She was either too stupid or too drunk to hear it. 'No offence, but Willa's not the type to find you on her own. She's a curious blend of timid and arrogant, shy and superior.'

Rob bit the inside of his lip to keep his words from stripping several layers of skin off her. He had a razor-sharp tongue and knew that he could inflict a cutting retort that would take her off at the knees. *Rein it in, bud. This isn't your fight and you don't need to make it worse for Willa than it already is.*

Tanned Plastic was trying to tap his mouth with her index finger and he yanked his head away just before she made contact.

'Anyway, I might have some use for your...*services.* Give me your mobile number so that I can contact you.'

Rob, his temper on a low simmer, sent her a bland look. 'Lady, I'd rather find a bathtub and chew my wrists off.'

Picking up his glass of whisky, he walked away from her fish face and walked up to Willa, who was still talking to their hosts.

'Nice friends you have,' he said to Misha, taking a sip of his whisky and welcoming its burn.

Willa gasped at his rudeness but, to his surprise, Misha just laughed.

'Dreadful aren't they? Especially Janice...that's who you were just talking to.'

Misha sent him a wide grin that he couldn't help returning.

'That's why we invited you, Willa. We wanted someone nice to talk to.'

So why have a fiftieth birthday party with people they didn't like? It didn't make sense, Rob thought—and then voiced his opinion out loud.

Instead of taking offence, Vern just shrugged. 'I believe in keeping my friends close and my enemies closer. So what do you do for a crust, Rob?'

'Janice thinks I'm a male escort,' Rob said blandly.

'Janice is a fool,' Misha replied. 'And desperately jealous of Willa.'

'She is not,' Willa protested.

'Of course she is,' Rob agreed. 'She's been throwing daggers at you all night. As are quite a few of the other women. You're at least twenty years younger than them, gorgeous, and most of the men here can't keep their eyes off you.'

'And why wouldn't they stare?' Vern said, lifting his glass to Willa. 'You look wonderful, my dear. Misha, there's the Thompsons—we should go say hello.' He looked at Rob. 'Enemies...'

'Do you have *any* friends here?' Rob asked.

Vern grinned. 'One or two. Look after Willa for us.'

'Will do.' Rob shook his head, puzzled, and looked down at Willa. 'What on earth does Vern do?'

'What doesn't he do?' Willa replied, lifting one bare shoulder. 'He's one of Australia's richest businessmen and he has interests in...well, literally everything. Hotels, mines, media, retail...'

Rob whistled his surprise. 'And your ex is a business associate of his?'

'Yeah.'

'Huh.'

So her ex swam in the same school as the big-boy fish? He'd be impressed but...he wasn't. Not by any of it. The yacht was swish, but the people were crappy, and the four-piece band playing in the corner was coma-inducing. The snacks were ordinary and he'd have more fun dodging taxi drivers in rush hour in downtown Jo'burg. He was bored, and when he was bored he tended to get into trouble by stirring up trouble.

'Can we go yet?' he asked, seeing that many eyes were still on them. He felt like an exhibit at a freak show.

Oh, well, might as well give them something they could really gossip about.

Rob bent his head and placed a long, sexy kiss on Willa's shoulder. When he lifted his head to look at her he saw that her eyes were smouldering with passion. Maybe they could find an empty bedroom—closet, bathroom—on this monstrous floating tub and have some fun.

'I want you,' he told her, sotto voce.

Willa licked her lips and he felt his blood rushing south.

'You always want me.'

'This is true.' He lifted her hand, opened her fingers and dropped an open-mouthed kiss on the centre of her palm. 'Is that a problem?'

'Yeah…kind of… Because when you look at me like that my knees go all wobbly and my vision blurs,' Willa admitted.

His ego puffed out its chest and did a high-five at the thought…

'And my panties get all wet.'

Okay, there went his knees. *Well-played, gorgeous.* 'Keep that up, honey, and I swear I'll give this room something more to talk about.'

Willa tipped her head. 'What would you do, Rob?'

Rob stepped up closer to her and his breath played with the hair at her ear. 'I'd run my hands up your stunning legs, pull that dress over your hips, push your thong aside and start moving.'

Willa kissed the side of his jaw. 'Panties now soaked—'

'You're making a spectacle of yourself, Willa. Stop it.'

Rob's hand fisted but he took his time moving away from Willa, dropping a brief but possessive kiss on her lips before pulling back and lifting his eyebrows at the balding blond man who was standing far too close to them, steam coming out of his ears. Okay, not literally, but still…

Rob didn't need his MBA to tell him that this was Wayne, Willa's soon-to-be ex-husband.

'Willa, do you *have* to embarrass me like this?' Wayne demanded. 'You're my *wife*, dammit!'

Rob opened his mouth to blast him but then remembered that Willa wanted to do this herself...recapture her pride and self-respect. He lifted an eyebrow at her but she wasn't looking at him. Her eyes were firmly on Wayne—a snake about to strike. She needed to handle this, he reminded himself. This was her party and he'd play bouncer—ready to step in if things got out of hand.

Wayne took a sip of whisky from his glass and his brows lifted to his receding hairline. 'What are you doing here anyway? These aren't *your* friends any more.'

Could he sound any more childish if he tried? God, what a moron. *Okay, Willa, any time now—blast him.* Rob placed a hand on her lower back and gave her an encouraging tap, but she just stood there, a fawn caught in the hunter's sights. He recognised that look. He had seen it on his mother's and sister's faces—probably on his own too.

'You've picked up some weight since I last saw you. You really should monitor your ice cream intake. Your backside is getting *huge*,' Wayne stated, his eyes glinting with malicious amusement.

Rob *so* wanted to punch him. For a moment he saw Stefan in Wayne's face and knew that he was dealing with the same type of character, the same need to control.

He rubbed his hand over his face. If he had to get involved with a woman, why couldn't it be with one who didn't make him feel as if he was reliving his past? Why did she have to be the one person he could thoroughly understand—who could probably understand him? He was already having problems keeping his emotional distance from her—how was he supposed to keep her at arm's length knowing just how miserable her last eight years must have been? Why couldn't she just have had an ex she'd fallen out of love with? Was that too much to ask?

The universe, he decided, had a sick sense of humour sometimes.

Rob noticed that they were attracting the attention of the rest of the room and decided that enough was enough. He couldn't stand here while the woman he...whatever he felt for Willa...was insulted and disparaged. He'd done that before and he'd never allow it to happen again.

'Back off, dude. Now,' he growled in Wayne's direction.

Wayne turned his attention to him and Rob held his shark-like eyes. Soft, mean and dangerous, he thought. But one punch to that jaw or a hook into his sternum would have him out cold or gasping like a fish. Lovely image, that.

'Who the hell are *you*? Did she hire you for the evening?' Wayne demanded.

Rob rolled his eyes at Misha and Vern who, obviously hoping to avoid blood on their expensive teak floors, had scuttled up to them. 'Nice to know that if the gyms and clothing line don't work out I have another option.'

Misha's eyes glinted with amusement. 'It's always good to have a Plan B. Wayne—really? Another scene?'

'We're still married, Michelle.'

Misha sent him a look to pin him to the floor. 'And where *is* your current lady-love, Wayne, darling? Oh, look.' She tapped the face of her disgustingly expensive diamond-studded bracelet watch and smiled brightly. 'It's after nine so it's probably past her curfew.'

'Not funny,' Wayne muttered.

Rob grinned at Misha. 'I thought it was. Didn't you, Willa?'

He sighed. Willa was still doing her 'see no evil, speak no evil and hear no evil' thing.

The rest of the room remained silent, Rob noticed, enthralled by the drama. Misha, obviously trying to rescue the situation, turned back to Wayne.

'Rob was telling me earlier that he owns a couple of fitness centres in South Africa as well as a chain of sports stores. He's expanding his business to Sydney, then Perth and Melbourne.'

'Interesting,' Vern murmured. 'A little risky when you have competition from Just Fit?'

Rob nodded. 'I've had two business consultants plus Willa look over the market research. They all agree that there's a gap in the market.'

'Like *Willa* knows anything about market research,' Wayne mocked. 'She's nothing but a pretty empty shell.'

'Careful,' Rob warned him. 'That's my accountant you're talking about.'

Wayne's eyes widened with astonishment and then he erupted into laughter. 'Oh, come on—you're kidding, right? You hired her as your *accountant*? You're stupider than you look!'

Rob flicked a glance at Willa, who still stood staring at Wayne, face ashen and eyes wide with hurt confusion. *Dammit, say something, Willa,* he urged her silently. *Take control, don't let this moron win.*

Rob squeezed her hand and she looked at him. He tipped his head in Wayne's direction, his eyes urging her to take a verbal swing. 'I've got your back,' he mouthed.

Willa took a deep breath, and he wondered if she knew that when she spoke her low, quiet, controlled voice had more power than shouting and screaming.

'I actually don't care what you think about me any more because you mean absolutely nothing to me. You didn't want a wife. You wanted a blow-up doll—someone who would feed your ego and tell you how wonderful you are. Except that you *aren't* wonderful...you're a sad man who gets his kicks from putting people down. And I am done with you.'

Yeah, you go, girl. Rob waited for her to say more but she just kept her eyes on Wayne's face, looking classy and strong and proud.

Rob couldn't help adding his two cents because—well, he wasn't going away without taking a couple of swings himself. Verbal only, of course. He looked Wayne in the eye and used his toughest, hardest, don't-mess-with-me voice.

'You must be a special kind of stupid not to realise how bright Willa actually is. She has a mind like a steel trap and she has the credentials to back it up. Smart and sexy... What kind of man would let *that* go?'

'I made her. I gave her everything!' Wayne spluttered, his face mottling instantly.

Typical bully—stand up to them and they back down... fast. The fact that he had six inches, ten years and twenty pounds of muscle on Wayne also helped.

'You gave her nothing of value.' Rob shook his head. 'She wasted far too much time on you...and now she's done.'

He deliberately turned his back to Wayne and stood in between him and Willa—a silent but, he hoped, an effective insult.

He winked at Willa and held out his hand. 'Ready to blow this joint, honey?'

'*So* ready.' Willa slid her much smaller hand into his.

He lifted his head at his hosts. 'Thanks, Misha and Vern... I wish I could say it's been fun.'

Vern grinned as he shook Rob's hand. 'I like you...come back.'

Rob shook his head. 'Nah, life is too short to spend my leisure time with people I don't like.'

Vern, instead of being insulted, just nodded. 'You may be right, son.'

'Happy birthday anyway.'

Rob tugged Willa and wrapped his arm around her slim waist. He bent his head to speak in her ear.

'So, where were we before we were so annoyingly interrupted...? Oh, I was sliding on in and your legs were wrapped around my hips...'

CHAPTER EIGHT

WILLA LOOKED ABSOLUTELY SHATTERED, and for that Rob wanted to go back onto that fancy yacht and pitch her waste-of-oxygen ex over the side. The funny, charming, sexy woman he'd spent the last few weeks with was gone and he was furious that the moron had wiped away her self-confidence, her happiness.

He looked sideways at her and thought that she looked like a 'roo in the headlights of a road train. Unfortunately he understood how deeply the scars of emotional abuse ran. He was proud of her, but she didn't seem to understand how far she'd come. Sure, she hadn't said much, but she'd said *something*.

It didn't matter that her words had just bounced off Wayne and that he'd only sat up and taken notice when Rob took him to task. None of that mattered because Willa had stood up for herself and he was proud of her. Yeah, he'd jumped in and got all he-man and protective, but he knew, deep down, that if hadn't been there Willa would have been just fine.

Eventually.

'So, on a scale of one to Chinese water torture, how much fun was *that*?' Rob asked as he opened the passenger door to her Mercedes, gesturing her inside.

Willa looked up at him, the sheen in her eyes suggesting tears. 'I'm so sorry.'

Rob slammed her car door shut and stalked around to the driver's seat, sliding inside and sending her a puzzled look. 'What exactly are you sorry for, Willa?'

'For everything. For even asking you to go.'

'You didn't ask me. I volunteered. Try again.' Rob started the car, pulled off, and flicked her another look. 'Put your seat belt on, honey.'

Willa just looked at him, so Rob leaned across her, pulled the strap from the harness across her body and snapped the lock into place.

'I put you in a silly situation and we had the attention of the entire room on us.'

As if he cared about that. 'I couldn't give a monkey's if all of Sydney was watching us,' Rob growled. Knowing that he'd sounded harsh, he placed a warm, large hand on her knee and tried to dial it down. 'Willa, I don't care what people think of me—I do not live my life wondering how to please other people and meet their expectations.'

'But you think I do,' Willa stated quietly.

'Actually, I think you were pretty amazing tonight.'

Willa snorted her disbelief. 'All I feel is humiliated. And stupid.'

'You don't have to feel that way.'

'I stood there with a mouth full of teeth and when I finally said something it was a couple of sentences that he hardly bothered to pay attention to.'

'That doesn't matter.'

'He didn't hear me or care!'

'And that's on him—not you. You did what you needed to do.'

Rob squeezed her knee again and wished he could pull over to take her in his arms, to offer the comfort he knew she so desperately needed. She was the only woman who had ever made him want to offer tenderness, to become involved. And it scared the hell out of him.

But worrying about how emotionally tied up he was becoming with this woman was for later... He was a man. He couldn't multitask.

He saw the stubborn tilt to her wobbly chin and gave it another shot. 'Where did you get this idea that you aren't entitled to express your feelings? Earlier you said that you didn't want them to remember you as a wimpy wife or as an easily dismissed insecure girl. You were talking about taking back your pride and self-respect.' Rob flicked her a glance. 'You did that.'

'Not very well,' Willa muttered. 'I got scared.'

'You didn't—don't—need to be. He's a wimpy moron in an expensive suit.' Rob kept his voice low and tried for soothing. He didn't know if he'd reached it…he'd never aimed for soothing before. 'I was standing right behind you. I wouldn't have allowed him to get close enough to touch you.'

Willa closed her eyes. 'I wasn't that type of scared. I felt myself sliding back into the person I was with Wayne—anxious to please, nervous, compliant—and that terrified me. What if this is who I actually am? Who, underneath it all, I'll always be?'

Yeah, he could understand that. He'd watched her sliding away tonight, back into a place where nothing and nobody could touch her. The person she was with him—cheeky, mischievous, confident—had disappeared at Wayne's first insult and she'd frozen, unable to get her vocal cords to move. Wayne had put her there, back in the life she'd hated, the state she'd hated, with a couple of well-placed barbs.

Seriously, he could still turn this car around and rearrange Wayne's face.

'I feel weak and foolish and sad.'

Rob placed his hand on her thigh and squeezed. 'You really don't need to.'

Willa looked out of the window as Rob turned into her driveway. He stopped the car, rested his arms on the steering wheel and looked out onto the dark night before reaching into his suit pocket to pull out his mobile.

'What are you doing?' she asked, her heart in her throat.

'Calling a taxi,' Rob answered quietly.

'You don't have to go.'

'Yeah, I think I do.' Rob looked at her with hot eyes. 'I think we should give each other a little space right now.' He shook his head as panic skittered across her face. 'Willa, get a grip!' *Tender, Hanson, remember to be tender.* He dropped his voice. 'I'm suggesting a night apart—that's it. Some time for me to work off the fact that I want to use your ex as a punchbag and some time for you to work through what happened tonight.'

Willa let out a long, relieved breath. 'Okay…but don't call a taxi. Take this car. I don't need it.'

'You sure?' Rob asked her.

'Yeah.' Willa opened the passenger door and looked at Rob, her battered heart in her eyes. 'I'm sorry I disappointed you.'

Rob rubbed his forehead with his fingers. 'Honey, that's just it. Either I'm not explaining this well or you're not hearing me but you damn well *didn't*.'

Rob let himself into Willa's house courtesy of the key he'd found in her sports car and wondered what he should do, say, to make things right. This was completely uncharted territory for him, he admitted, heading for the kitchen, where he could hear music playing from the retro radio on the long shelf next to the door.

He only ever dated, slept with, strong women, confident women—women who knew who they were and what they wanted. *How would you know what they wanted?* he asked himself mockingly. *You never stuck around long enough to ask or to find out whether their confidence was a shield or their strength was faked.*

Willa was strong, he admitted. You couldn't survive a controlling marriage, get your degree and then find the guts to leave if you weren't. If he had to judge only by last night's response, then he might have to say that she was weak and easily cowed, but last night she hadn't been the same person she was with him. With him she was sharper, funnier, stronger, chirpier.

Who was the real Willa? Maybe she was still too fragile? Maybe she needed someone…different? Better? He was impatient and gruff and forthright—too damn honest for most people, especially women, to handle. He was sometimes brutal, always clear-thinking and matter-of-fact; he called things as he saw them.

The thought of her being with anyone else made him want to put his hand through the wall, but despite his caveman response—and what was *that* about?—he knew that the right thing to do was to back away, to give her space. Which posed a problem since, A. She was working for him, and B. He didn't want to.

Rob poured two cups of coffee and took them to the office, where he'd expected Willa to be. Not finding her behind her desk, he stepped through the door of the study onto the veranda and found her sitting on the edge of the pool, her feet in the water.

Hearing his footsteps, she lifted her face. He wished that she wasn't wearing huge sunglasses that dominated her face; he wanted to see her eyes. Firstly because looking into Willa's eyes was always a pleasure, but mostly because then he could read, so clearly, what was troubling her.

'Take your shades off for a moment.'

'Why?'

'Please?'

Willa shrugged and pushed her glasses up into her hair. He scanned her face, her eyes, and, yep, there they were. Anger, humiliation, sadness.

'Here.'

Willa took the cup he held out with murmured thanks

and Rob lowered himself to sit next to her, taking the sunglasses off the top of his own head and sliding them onto his face. He slipped hers back onto her nose.

'You okay?' he asked, when she didn't say anything at all.

'Still feeling like a fool,' Willa admitted quietly.

'What for? For not saying more or for marrying that moron? Or for going to that party in the first place?' Rob asked. *Yeah, too honest.*

'All of the above,' Willa stated. 'God, this coffee is good—but it would've been better with a doughnut. I'm starving.'

'Well, you didn't eat anything on the yacht last night.'

'Catamaran.' Willa saw the look he sent her and shrugged. 'It was a catamaran...two hulls...not a yacht. Just being accurate.'

'I'm a city boy. I know Jack about yachts and boats,' Rob replied. 'So, are we going to talk about last night?'

'It's such a gorgeous day,' Willa said, looking past him to the harbour in the distance, the gentle waters of the bay below them. Rob was back and her world made sense again.

'Nice try, but we're not changing the subject.'

Willa sighed as she recognised the stubborn look in his eye. 'I've said, over and over, that I feel a fool! Especially since I know that he's a balding bully—a little man with a big ego that needs to be fed.' Willa put her cup down on the pavement, looking anguished. 'Why couldn't I say more?'

'Had you seen him since you separated?'

Willa shook her head. 'Only in meetings with Kate, and then she and his lawyer did most of the talking.' She sighed and leaned back. 'I suppose you think that's stupid?'

Rob tapped his finger against the mug he held. 'No, not stupid.'

'I'm so angry with myself because I've worked so hard over the last months to stop believing the crap he fed me about myself. I've been telling myself that I was young and impressionable, that I didn't have anyone in my life to counter his opinion, and that that time is over—*he* is over. I believed that. But then he was there and I went straight back into stupid mode.'

'Habit reaction. It's classic abuse-sufferer behaviour,' Rob murmured.

'He didn't abuse me…' Willa protested.

'Verbal abuse is still abuse and it's just as dangerous. Bet he also played the blame game and the silent game and the can't-please-me game as well.'

'You sound like you know what you're talking about.'

'I *do* know what I'm talking about,' Rob admitted reluctantly. 'My stepfather abused my mother and my sister for three years until my uncle put a stop to it.'

Willa bit her bottom lip in sympathy. 'I'm so sorry. How…?' Her heart bled for him, for the pain she could still see in his eyes, the bleakness in his voice. 'I'm not sure what to say…'

'Not a hell of a lot *to* say. We were weak, still reeling from the death of my dad a year before, and Stefan was our rock, our comfort, my dad's best friend. He and my mum grew closer and she asked me if I thought she should marry him.'

'And you said yes?'

'I wanted her to be happy again and—' Rob abruptly stopped speaking, taking a sip of his coffee instead.

'And?' Willa prodded.

Rob stared at the bright blue pool. 'And I wanted to go off across country to study at uni. I could do that without guilt if I knew that he was looking after my mum and sister. Then he moved in and took over their lives…he made me what I am.'

'Which is?' Willa asked crisply.

'Generally flawed. Mostly distrustful. Of myself and

of everyone around me. Impatient, closed-off, unwilling to commit.'

'Why?'

'After my dad, Stefan was my hero. I genuinely respected him—loved him, even. I would never have thought that he would turn into an abusive bully. I learnt the hard way that what you see is never what you actually get.'

'"Impatient, closed-off, unwilling to commit..."' Willa tipped her head. 'Sounds like somebody made a list.'

'Many somebodys—all female, all mad when I dumped them.' Rob shrugged, looking resigned and then resolute. 'They weren't wrong, Willa.'

They'd forgotten to tell him that he was hard-working and sexy, honourable and loyal, had a wicked sense of humour and a protective instinct a mile long.

Rob lifted a powerful shoulder in an agitated shrug. 'The thing is...because I don't—*can't* trust, I don't have relationships. I have flings. When it starts getting a bit too real, I bail.'

Willa pulled in a deep breath, feeling compelled to ask, to find out exactly where she stood with him. 'Is *this* getting a bit too real? Are you wanting to bail?'

Rob twisted his lips. 'I'm thinking that if you were in an abusive relationship then I am exactly the wrong type of guy you should be having a rebound fling with. You need someone gentle, compassionate, patient. I'm none of those things...'

Willa was quiet for a moment, thinking about what he'd said. It wasn't as if she hadn't had the same thoughts a couple of times during the long night. A nice man would be easier, calmer—wouldn't force her to confront her demons, would let her ease into her new life. A gentle man would give her time and compassion...

Except that she didn't need time and compassion. She

needed a boot up the backside. She needed someone to yank her out of her 'woe is me' attitude and tell her to get a grip and get a life. There was something about Rob that inspired her to be tougher, stronger. Rob, just by being Rob, made her want to step up to the plate and take her best shot. To be brave enough to try.

He wasn't easy, but his attitude was good for her.

He was perfect for her right now. Maybe for ever. He didn't let her coast or cruise…

Willa pulled her glasses off her face and tapped them against her knee. 'No, you're not patient or gentle, but I know that you can be compassionate. And I don't need someone to pussyfoot around me. I've been protected and cosseted my whole life. I need a man who doesn't want to treat me like china—a man who demands that I stand on my own two feet, that I be a woman and start acting like one.'

'I call it like I see it. I always have…it's just who I am.'

'And I need someone in my life like that.'

Willa saw him mentally retreat, saw him back-pedalling and knew that this conversation had gone too deep, too quickly. Rob was looking panicked, and she wouldn't be surprised if he broke out in hives some time soon.

Relax, Rob, it's all still good, she wanted to tell him. Despite this conversation she knew that it was just surface, just temporary between them.

Because he was looking faintly green, she gave him some breathing room. 'I'd like you to carry on being your gruff self for as long as you're here—even if it that is only for a couple more days, weeks… When *are* you heading back to South Africa?'

Relief loosened that tight, ticking muscle in his jaw, the tense cords of his neck, and she vaguely listened to him explain that he might be here for three more weeks, a month at the most, quickly understanding that this was still very much just a fling for him.

Willa bit the inside of her lip.

Unfortunately she was starting to feel that, for her, maybe it wasn't any more.

Willa looked around the dining table at her friends and wished Brodie had accepted her invitation to dinner, although she'd never expected him to. Seeing Rob and Scott deep in conversation about an architect she'd never heard of reminded her of how well Scott and Brodie had got along—how they'd have those same masculine, short-sentence conversations that went on for hours.

She liked having people around her table…liked being able to feed them, cook for them. A simple meal. Chicken pasta and salad. Garlic bread. Good wine from the cellar downstairs. Excellent company.

Talking of which, she wished Kate was here, but she, like Brodie, supposedly had to work. Amy was here, and Jessica had brought along the Weeping Reef ex-lifeguard she'd left with the other day and the six of them had laughed and chattered through dinner and more than a few bottles of wine from the cellar.

She had a lot to be grateful for…

She should be happy…

She was having explosive sex with a man who excelled at the art, she had reconnected with her friends and she had a job that challenged her on every level. So why was she feeling out of sorts, dissociated, unsettled?

Willa left her friends talking and picked up some empty plates and took them to the kitchen. Wanting a minute to herself, she looked out of the kitchen window as she held on to the granite edge of the counter. She'd come so far in eight months; she should be incredibly proud of herself…

Should be…should be…should be…

But what had she done, really? She'd walked away from her sucky marriage…big deal. That was nothing in the scheme of things; women defied governments, defended their countries, fought poverty and sexism and lack of education all over the world. Her leaving Wayne wasn't exactly behaviour worthy of admiration—especially since it had been about eight years overdue.

She was living in a mansion house that her ex had paid for, driving a car that her ex had paid for, and at the only opportunity she'd had to show Wayne—to show herself—that she was her own person, she'd blown it.

As for Rob…her one-night stand had turned into an affair with a sell-by date; she wasn't sure what that date was, but it would soon be over. And because she'd been desperate to work, and had begged him for the job, she'd landed her position as Rob's accountant by default too.

She was, basically, sleeping with her boss.

She hadn't pitted herself against any other applicants, she hadn't been measured against her peers. How could she be sure that she was as capable as them? That she had the job because she was actually good at it and not just good at the bedroom-based activities she engaged in with Rob?

Seeing an open bottle of red on the counter, she reached for a glass and poured herself a half-glass that she threw down her throat. He had an accountant and a lover…good deal for *him*.

Basically, she was still living her life according to other people's tenets: she'd been the good daughter, then the trophy wife, and now she was exactly what Rob wanted—his casual fling and his accountant.

What did she want, for God's sake? And was she ever going to start making decisions for herself?

Willa poured herself another glass of wine and sipped it slowly. Yeah, maybe it was about time she started doing exactly that.

* * *

Willa and Kate were lying on loungers in the late-afternoon sun, a pitcher of icy sangria between them, drying off after a refreshing swim. Kate pushed her designer sunglasses up on her face and rolled her head to look at Willa.

'Where's Hot and Spicy?'

Willa smiled at the moniker. 'He went to Brisbane for a couple of days. He's meeting with some people who want to buy into his franchise. Next week he's heading to Perth.'

'He looks too rough and ready to be such a hotshot businessman. He looks like he should be a rugby player or a surfer,' Kate stated idly.

'I know, right? But he's great at what he does. He's got brilliant instincts and great vision—though he's not wild about the accountancy side of the business,' Willa said, thinking that getting Rob to discuss VAT and tax was akin to pulling teeth.

'And that's why he hired you.' Kate rolled over onto her side and rested her head in her hand. 'How's that working for you?'

'I love it...' Willa replied. 'I love making numbers dance.'

Kate pulled a face. 'I'm with Rob on the hating accountancy part...I find it deeply boring. And are you managing to work together *and* sleep together?'

Willa looked out onto the harbour. 'Rob makes the transition a lot easier than I do. He flips a switch and instantly forgets that we've just had an argument about cash flow and staff benefits. I take a lot longer to...transition.'

'Rob understands that there's nothing personal in the argument but you don't seem to,' Kate commented. 'It's something that comes with experience. Give it time and you'll get there.'

Willa refilled their glasses with sangria and handed Kate hers. She tapped her nails against the icy glass... She needed to talk to somebody about Rob and since Kate was now her closest friend she was duly elected. 'I'm feeling really confused, Kate, and slightly at sea.'

Kate sat up straight and pulled her sunglasses off her face. She scanned Willa's face before asking, 'Okay…why?'

Willa took a sip of her drink before putting the glass on the table between them. The sun had started falling in the sky and was turning from gold to orange. 'When I got over the shock of living on my own, without Wayne, I promised myself that I would do what I wanted to do and what I felt was right—for me.'

Kate didn't respond, just cocked her head in interest.

'I was just getting to a point in my life when I felt like I was coming into my own, being me, and I fell into bed with Rob.'

'Mmm-hmm. And the problem is…?' Kate placed her elbows on her crossed knees and cupped her face in her hands.

Willa huffed out her breath. 'I'm not even sure if there is a problem or whether I'm just making problems…' she admitted, now wishing that she hadn't opened this can of worms.

'Just spit it out, Willa.'

'I still feel mortified that I clammed up when Wayne insulted me in front of all those people. Rob was there, but I just stood there and got…scared, stupid. It was like stepping back into being that downtrodden, subservient wife I had been and I hated it! My words dried up and all I wanted to do was run away from him, as far and as fast as I could. Rob had to stick up for me.'

'But you *did* speak.'

'I didn't say enough,' Willa stated.

'It's okay, Willa. Stop being so hard on yourself.'

Kate didn't look outraged or even disappointed. Easy for Kate to say, but Willa didn't want to be the subservient, meek, timid woman she was with Wayne; she wanted to be bold and fierce and confident—all the time!

'You've come a long, long way, Willa. Don't lose sight of that just because you had a setback with The Pain.'

But maybe she hadn't come as far as Kate thought—as far as she'd believed she had. Her life had changed so dramatically and she was having difficulty processing all the changes. She was still getting used to being on her own, coming to terms with the demise of her marriage and the part she'd played in it. Sure, Wayne was an idiot of extraordinary skill, but she'd *allowed* him to treat her like that; by not fully standing up to him she'd given him permission to treat her badly.

He'd called all the shots in her marriage and her life and... Willa rubbed her hands over her face. And she was scared that she was allowing history to repeat itself.

Rob was, to an extent, calling all the shots in this relationship. He was a force of nature and she was in danger of being swept away by the strength of his personality. He'd fallen into her bed and fallen into her life and now he was her boss.

Holy hell, what had she jumped into here? Had she gone straight from the frying pan into—well, the sixty-fourth level of hell? Had she been blinded by Rob's handsome face and luscious body and his ability to give her mind-blowing orgasms? Was she that weak, that shallow, that starved for attention?

What did she want? What did she deserve?

Surely it was more than this?

'Oh, fudge,' Kate said, scrunching up her eyes.

'What?' Willa asked.

'That look on your face—I recognise it as your Willa-digging-her-heels-in look.' Kate stood up and knotted her wrap on her right hip.

Willa smiled reluctantly. 'Am I that transparent?'

'Sorry…but, yes. What are you thinking about, honey?'

Willa adjusted the cups of her strapless pink bikini. 'I'm thinking that it's time I worked out exactly what I want from life and men…and Rob. I need to start deciding what is right for *me*.'

Kate placed a hand on her chest and wiped away an imaginary tear. 'My baby girl is finally growing up.'

Willa didn't have a verbal comeback so she placed her hands on Kate's shoulders and pushed her into the pool.

CHAPTER NINE

'You bitch!'

Willa, barrelling up the steps to the front door after her early-morning run, jumped a foot in the air as Wayne stepped out of the shadows of the veranda, a menacing look on his face.

Recognising that he had a major temper brewing, she slapped a hand on her chest and closed her eyes. *Not now*, she prayed. She was so close to being free of him. Why was he here? What did he want?

'How dare you embarrass me in front of my friends, my business associates last week? Everyone was laughing at me behind my back!' Wayne hissed. 'Vern cancelled a deal with me yesterday—said that he didn't like the way I treated you. You stupid bitch.'

And this was *her* fault? How? Willa desperately wanted to tell him not to call her names, that he was no longer allowed to do that, but seeing the cold fury in his eyes had sent her words and her courage belting away. Again.

And she'd seen Wayne angry before, but she'd never seen that sadistic gleam in his eyes. 'You think you're so smart, with your hulk boyfriend protecting you, but I'm not done with you. I'm not done showing you how useless I think you are… *I'm not done*.'

Willa bit her lip and thought that she had to get away. She moved to the right but Wayne blocked her escape down the path to the road. She was trapped… God, why she had allowed Rob to go back to his flat last night? If Rob was here then Wayne wouldn't be doing this... Then again, Wayne was a coward. He had to know that Rob wasn't here...

Dear God, she was on her own.

'Calm down, Wayne.'

Wayne gripped the top parts of her arms and his fingers dug in. Willa winced, but didn't attempt to remove herself from his grasp.

'I will not calm down, bitch. I am so goddamn angry with you... You will not defy me; you will not make me look stupid. I will bloody teach you this lesson if it's the last thing I do. Open the door and get inside.'

Oh, crap, she was in bigger trouble here than she'd thought.

Willa fought down the urge to panic and ignored the pain of his fingers digging into her arms. If she let him into the house she would be at his mercy...but if she didn't he might just start hitting her here.

Because being hit was in her immediate future. She knew that as well as she knew her own name. He'd never done it before, but losing face with Vern would have pushed him over the edge. Wayne, being the narcissistic ass that he was, would always find someone else to blame.

Willa froze, every muscle in her body tensing. She wanted to fight him but she was so damn scared. She wanted to scream at him but knew that would just make him madder. She was trapped...

This was how Amy had felt, she thought. Terrified and alone... She remembered Amy's bruises and injuries and she shuddered. *Oh, Ames...*

'Open the bloody door or I swear I'll just make it worse.'

Wayne shook her and Willa reached for the key. Maybe if she just listened to him he would come to his senses and she'd escape with nothing more than a slap...

Don't go in the house, Willa. Fight.

Willa felt her anger swell and her courage return with

the force of a tidal wave. She was not doing this again—
she was not going to be Wayne's wimpy wife ever again!

Whirling around, she slapped both her hands on Wayne's
chest and, shoving as hard as she could, pushed him back a
couple of steps. She'd never, as long as she lived, forget the
astonished look on his face. It gave her even more courage.

'You want to take a swing at me? You do it right here,
you bastard!'

Wayne's eyes widened and Willa saw his fist clench.
Instead of retreating, Willa got in his face.

'But you should know that I'll fight back, I'll fight you
with everything I have! And if you touch me you'd better
kill me because I swear to God I will nail your saggy ass
to a wall when I charge you with assault,' she hissed.

Wayne stopped in his tracks and looked at her, hesitat-
ing. Willa felt her power surge again and she knew she
wasn't nearly done with him. She had no back-up but she
didn't need it...not this time.

She was Willa Moore, and she was going to take control of her life, dammit!

'You will never disparage me, insult me or put me down
again! You will never threaten me with violence, put your
hands on me or make me feel less than I am.' Willa's chest
heaved with anger and her eyes were laser-sharp.

'Willa, calm down...'

Willa actually growled at him. 'Don't you *dare* tell me
what to do! God *damn* you! You complete bastard moron!'

Wayne looked around and started inching his way towards the steps. 'I think that you should—'

He was still talking? Really? Well, it wasn't his time to
talk, it was hers. She had eight years' worth of anger needing an escape and he was in her target zone.

'I actually don't care what you think I should do, you
spineless, pathetic, shiny-headed weasel. I'm not a little girl
any more. Come to think of it, why can't you have relation-

ships with women who are women and not girls, Wayne? Are you that insecure?'

Willa gave him half a second to answer before storming in again.

'Are you threatened by women being smarter, older? Do you see young girls as women you can mould? Are you just sick? I had so much to give, dammit, and you stifled me at every turn—'

'I wanted to protect you!' Wayne protested.

'You wanted to control me and, well done, you succeeded…for a while.' Willa shoved her hands into her hair and tugged. 'But I've escaped your saggy clutches now, you horrible man, and I won't be made to feel bad about it—especially not by you.'

'Hey, Willa. Morning!'

They both whirled around and Willa saw her sprightly neighbours, Jerry and Luella, at the bottom of her driveway, their Alsatian Ben between them. She finally had Wayne on the back foot, she had so much more grief to give him, and she was being interrupted. Wayne, the soft, yellow-bellied coward, looked relieved.

Jerry frowned when Willa didn't respond, and he and Ben walked towards her up the path. Ben growled and Jerry looked from Willa to Wayne.

'Everything okay here?'

Wayne looked even more relieved. 'I'm just leaving.'

Willa saw the enquiring look Jerry sent her and shrugged. 'My revolting ex.'

Jerry, six two and still powerful, despite being in his sixties, crossed his tree trunk arms and glared at Wayne. 'We'll just wait until you do just that.'

Ben went to sit next to Willa's legs and growled when Wayne took a half-step towards her. Wayne muttered an obscenity, sent Willa a furious look, and when neither she nor Jerry—nor Ben—moved he whirled away and stomped down the driveway.

Jerry waited until he saw Wayne roar off in his Ferrari before he placed a meaty hand on Willa's shaking shoulder. 'You okay, hun? He looked like a nasty piece of work.'

Willa released the breath she was holding. 'He is. But today—' she grinned at him '—I was nastier. Thanks, Jerry.' She rubbed Ben between the ears. 'You too, Ben.'

Jerry took the key from her shaking hand, put it in the lock and pushed her door open for her. 'Lock it behind you and be careful. Where's that nice guy who's been hanging around?'

'Rob?' Willa pushed her hand through her hair. 'He'll be around later.'

'Good.' Jerry pushed her inside. 'Take care and call me if the other guy comes back.'

'Thanks, Jerry.'

Willa blew him a kiss, slipped inside her house, closed the door and locked it. Leaning against the door, she slid to the floor, wrapped her arms around her knees and cried.

She shouldn't be crying, Willa thought, brushing at her tears. She'd fought the monster under her bed, the one inside her head, and she'd won. She should be laughing, dancing, celebrating…

She had her self-respect back. She hadn't disappointed herself again. She'd fought back. So why was she crying?

Cleansing tears, she realised eventually. Facing Wayne down had been like removing a festering thorn: the irritant was out, but there was still some muck in the hole.

So Willa, her back to the door and her head on her knees, allowed herself to cry. To be cleansed.

When Rob got to Willa's at midday he had to wait while she answered the front door, which for once was locked. Silently, he followed her stiff back to the study. He had enough experience with women to realise that something was amiss, and he ran back through their last couple of conversations to see if he'd put his foot in it or forgotten something important… He couldn't think of anything in particular, but who knew?

Maybe it wasn't him… Maybe she'd had a fight with one of her girlfriends—or might she be getting sick? Did she look a little red? Rob shook his head at the urge to place the back of his hand against her forehead to see if she was running a temperature.

He was, he was humiliated to admit, a sap. Why did he care so much? He was just here, with her, for a little company, a lot of sex. Some laughs…

He wasn't here to fix her, protect her, look after her. That wasn't his job.

Willa, dressed in a pair of cut-off jeans and a long-sleeved tee—it was about a million degrees outside…why the long sleeves?—walked around her desk and sank into her chair.

'We need to go through the cost projections for the store and the cash-flow projections for the gym,' Willa said crisply, looking at her computer screen. 'Let me just print them out.'

Rob frowned, conscious of the fact that Willa hadn't yet met his eyes. He peered into her face, noticing that she looked a little pale. Hell, maybe she *was* getting sick…

'Hey, are you okay?'

'I'm fine,' she snapped.

Okay, then, bite my head off, why don't you?

'You're looking out of sorts and you're wearing sleeves on a steaming hot day. Are you getting sick?' Rob persisted.

'Maybe.' Willa gestured to her desk. 'Can we get to work, please?'

'No.' Rob walked around the desk, lifted her chin and

looked into her unhappy red-rimmed eyes. 'Have you been crying?'

'Rob, enough! I just want to get to work; we have so much to do!'

Rob placed his hands on the armrests of her chair and shook his head. 'Firstly, it's Sunday—and it's against my religion to work on a Sunday.'

Willa snorted. 'What religion is that? Paganism?'

'And secondly something big is bothering you.'

Rob placed his hands on her arms and his blood froze when she let out a smothered yelp of pain. Instinctively he recognised that sound: the sound of someone—a woman… *his* woman!—trying to hide an injury. Dropping her back into her chair, he swiftly reached for the hem of her T-shirt and tugged it up.

'What are you doing? I'm not getting naked right now!'

'Take the T-shirt off, Willa,' Rob stated, his voice low and hard. His tone suggested that she did not argue with him.

Willa's voice broke. 'Please, Rob, just let it go.'

Like hell. 'Off. Now.'

He tugged the hem of the shirt again and, feeling the resistance leave her, gently pulled the T-shirt over her head. His eyes scanned her torso and then he saw the purple, perfect bruises that indicated fingers holding her left arm far too tight. His eyes jumped to her other arm where she had a matching set.

'When was he here?' he growled, stepping back and looking at her through a red mist of temper. He had to control it this one time. He had to be better than he was.

'It's nothing—'

'It's something, Willa. Let's have it,' Rob said, struggling to keep his composure.

'Early this morning,' Willa admitted reluctantly. 'He was waiting for me when I came back from my run.'

Willa yanked her T-shirt out of his hands and pulled it over her head. Somewhere, in the place that wasn't all caveman, he realised that her voice radiated frustration and temper but no timidity.

'He said that I'd embarrassed him and he was going to teach me a lesson... I think if he'd got me into the house then he would've slapped me around.'

Rob felt his gut clench and nausea roil through him. He breathed through his nose and ordered his stomach to settle down. 'Dear God...'

The words were more of a plea than a blasphemy.

'For far too many minutes I just stood there...couldn't fight him. Couldn't say a damn thing... I've never seen him look like that... I was so scared.' Willa wrapped her arms around her middle and dropped her head.

Rob couldn't comfort her—he was too angry. Instead he pivoted on his heel and slammed his fist into a wooden cupboard behind him. Willa gasped, and fire rocketed up his arm, but it was worth it because for a moment—just a moment—he imagined that it was Wayne Fisher's face on the other side of his fist.

Then he rested his head against the cupboard as he pulled in deep breaths, grateful that the punch had taken the edge off. When he thought he could face her again with a measure of calm, he turned around.

Willa's mouth had dropped open and he was, on one level, pleased to see a spark back in her eyes.

'Was that necessary? Jeez—calm down, Rob.'

He was calm. Just... But he was still in the zone. To prove his point, if only to himself, he lowered his voice even further. 'He put his hands on you...he was going to beat you—terrorise you! I'm trying, very hard, to stop myself from going caveman.'

'I *handled* him!' Willa cried. 'If you could pull your head out of your ass for five seconds and concentrate, you'd actually hear what is important here! I stood up to him—without you, I might add. I tore into him and it felt brilliant! This isn't your problem, Rob!' she stated, leaning forward. 'He's my ex-husband, my problem, my issue! He pushed and I pushed back harder! He left with his tail between his legs...'

Rob stared at a spot on the wall past her head, his back teeth grinding together. At this rate he might have to get them crowned. 'I should've been here...'

'I'm glad you weren't,' Willa admitted candidly, and rolled her eyes at his ferocious scowl. 'I needed to do that, Rob! I needed to take him on, to fight back—'

'You could've made it worse.'

'Coulda, woulda, shoulda... I *didn't*! He backed down and he'll never try that again.'

'You hope. Still, if I'd been here...'

'If you'd been here I might have let you handle him—but *I* needed to. Can't you understand that?' Willa sighed and rubbed her hands over her face.

'He put bruises on your arms and he made you cry,' Rob stated in a bleak voice.

'The bruises will fade and I cried because I felt like this huge weight was finally off my shoulders.' Willa stood up, took a step towards him and wrapped her arms around his neck, burying her face in his chest. 'I need you to let this go. I was getting there, and now I'm upset because *you're* upset. He's not worth it, Rob.'

Rob allowed himself to run his uninjured hand down her back. 'He can't be allowed to get away with threatening you; that's not acceptable, Wills.'

'I'll tell Kate. She'll know what to do,' Willa conceded and Rob felt his temper start to drain away.

'Call her now,' he insisted.

Willa nodded and dropped her arms. She lifted his hand

and winced at his scraped and swelling knuckles. 'Oh, Rob, dammit. This needs ice.'

Rob looked at his hand and shrugged. He couldn't feel anything at the moment—adrenalin was keeping the pain at bay—but he knew that in an hour or so he'd be feeling the effects of punching a solid oak cabinet.

He slid a glance to the cupboard, where a fist-sized dent was impossible to miss. 'Sorry, Willa, I've ruined it.'

'I don't give a damn about the cupboard; I'm just worried that you've broken some fingers!'

Rob wiggled his fingers and felt pain shooting up his hand. *Hellfire and all its demons.* 'Not broken.'

'You need an ice pack.' Willa dropped his hand and rested her forehead against his chest. 'Despite the fact that you went all Neanderthal on me, I'm so glad you're here now, Rob.'

Rob wrapped his arms around her cold body and pulled her into him, trying to get her as close as possible. 'I should have decked him the other night, Wills.'

'He went home today feeling terrible, Rob. He heard me—he finally heard me. That's all that matters right now.'

An hour later Kate paced Willa's kitchen, an untouched cup of coffee in her hands, her mouth pursed and her eyes flashing with anger. She looked from Willa to Rob, who was holding a bag of peas against his now swollen hand, and back again.

'The problem is that he didn't actually *do* anything,' Kate said, having listened to Willa telling the story of her encounter with Wayne.

'He threatened her, Kate! Bruised her!'

'Rob, if the police arrested people on threats our jails would be jam-packed. And he could easily claim the bruises weren't caused by him,' Kate retorted. 'I want to tell you that there's something we can do but there isn't! Dammit.'

Rob just growled his displeasure.

Willa looked at her dark knight and swallowed her smile. She really believed that he and Kate were both overreacting. She knew Wayne and he was a consummate bully. He'd scuttled away from her and he wouldn't try anything ever again. He'd cut her out of his life, wouldn't acknowledge her ever again and she was *so* okay with that.

Rob, however, was still vibrating with suppressed anger. For her.

'I hear what you're saying, Kate, and I understand. Wayne was in a temper. He was furious that he'd lost the deal with Vern and it's in his nature to look for a scapegoat. I was it. He won't try this again...he can't afford to get arrested on a charge of assault.'

Kate nodded, finally took a sip of her now cold coffee and grimaced. 'I agree. However, I *will* be making a call to his attorney in a minute and I *will* tell him what happened this morning. I will also tell him that if his client comes within a hundred metres of you, I will take out a restraining order on your behalf. Will your neighbour back up your claims?'

'He can tell you that he was holding me and acting crazy and threatening,' Willa said.

'Good.'

Rob pulled out his mobile from his pocket and fiddled with the buttons. 'Take your T-shirt off, Willa.'

'Haven't we sung this song already today?' Willa complained.

'Photo evidence,' Rob replied, impatient.

'It's a good idea, Willa,' Kate agreed. 'I'll attach it to the follow-up e-mail I'll be sending his lawyer.'

'Dammit...' Willa muttered, and took her shirt off for the second time.

Rob's lips firmed and his jaw clenched as he lifted his mobile to photograph her arm. Willa looked down and grimaced. What had been faint blue smudges this morning were now livid purple bruises.

'Don't punch anything,' she warned Rob, who looked ready to do that again.

Rob glared at her as the phone's camera did its thing, and when he was finished he pushed his chair back from the table, handed Kate his mobile and stalked from the room.

Willa started to go after him but Kate's hand on her arm halted her flight across the room. 'He needs some time on his own, Willa. Leave him. He needs to work through his anger—to process what's happened.'

'He's so angry, Kate.'

'Of course he is; he wasn't able to protect you, and to an alpha male like Rob that is like a massive kick in the nuts by a little girl. Give him time, Wills. He'll come back when he's worked through it.'

Willa looked at Rob's disappearing back and remembered what he'd said about his stepfather—that he'd been abusive towards his mother. Maybe Wayne's crazy stunt had pulled a whole lot of memories and angst to the surface.

She suspected it might be a long time before he came to her...

If at all.

Taking Kate's advice, Willa left the brooding Rob alone and, thinking she needed something to take her mind off her crazy morning, decided to tackle the cost projections and cash-flow spreadsheets herself. Soon she was lost in the numbers, carried away with her work. Here there were no mad ex-husbands wanting to teach her a lesson, nor brooding part time lovers, there were just the numbers; straightforward and simple.

Rob pulled her back to the present by knocking his good fist on her desk.

Willa jerked her head up, pulled her glasses off and rubbed her eyes. 'Hi.'

'Hi back. I've made lunch,' Rob said. 'Take a break— you've been at it for four hours.'

'Ah...okay.' She stretched her spine before climbing to her feet and following Rob out to the veranda. On the wooden table he'd placed a huge seafood salad, plates, and an icy bottle of white wine. Willa instantly began to salivate.

Sliding onto the wooden bench, she reached for a plate and dumped the avocado and prawn-rich salad onto her plate. 'This looks *so* good.'

Rob poured wine into the glasses, handed hers over and took a seat opposite her. Willa saw that he was only using one hand and grimaced in sympathy. His other hand was swollen, black and blue.

'Is it very painful?'

Rob looked at his fingers and shrugged. 'I'll live.'

Boy-speak for, *Hell, yeah, it's sore.*

'I'd like to move in here. Is that okay with you?' Rob asked, his tone sober. 'I'm worried he'll come back.'

'I really don't think that is likely. Besides, I'll be divorced in a couple of weeks,' Willa responded, looking at her heaped fork.

'Say yes, Wills. Please?'

Willa mentally debated what to do. Rob was spending most nights with her anyway, and it was stupid him renting an apartment that he rarely occupied. And there was no doubt that she'd feel safer with him around...not that she needed to feel safe. She now knew that she could handle Wayne—once a day and twice on Sundays.

But she wanted Rob with her not as a guard dog or a sleeping aid but as the man she wanted in her life—as someone she wanted to spend as much time with as possible.

She wanted him to see her as his equal, as someone strong and capable, not as a weakling who needed his protection. She wanted him to *want* to be with her—not because he had a misplaced white knight complex.

'I don't need your pity or your protection, Rob,' she told him, after she'd forthrightly explained her dilemma.

Rob sat back in his chair and a glint of amusement sparked in his eyes. 'I like the set of teeth you've suddenly grown, Willa.'

Willa stared him down, unwilling to be distracted from the matter at hand, and Rob eventually lifted a hand in resignation. 'I'm by nature a protector, and I can't and won't apologise for that. I will always jump in front of the bus, the bullet, the wild pack of hyenas. But I don't pity you. I don't believe in pity.' He flashed her his panty-melting grin. 'And I like the idea of being able to fool around whenever and wherever we please.'

'We're doing that already,' Willa pointed out, sure that he was trying to bamboozle her.

'Yeah, but occasionally I still drive to the flat at night— a danger to all road-users as my mind is usually still in bed with you.'

Willa narrowed her eyes at him as she fought a grin. 'You are *so* full of it. Okay,' she said, before she forked her salad into her mouth. 'Move in.' Her eyes twinkled for the first time that day. 'There are many guest bedrooms to choose from.'

'Ha-ha, funny girl.' Rob narrowed his eyes at her. 'The only place I am sleeping is next to you.'

'We won't get a lot of sleeping done,' Willa told him, her lips curving in anticipation.

Rob looked at her quizzically. 'And why,' he asked in that sexy drawl, 'would *that* be a problem?'

Rob, coming up from Willa's gym, rubbing his sweaty face and bare chest with a towel, stopped abruptly when he heard voices in the formal lounge.

Poking his head around the doorframe, he saw Willa, dressed in a pencil skirt that ended a couple of inches above her knees and a formal business jacket that he hated. Her fabulous hair was pulled into a tight knot at the back of her head and she was having an earnest discussion with two men in sharp suits. The younger held a tablet and was making notes in between sneaking looks at Willa's legs. Although Rob didn't like it, he couldn't blame him—he liked Willa's legs too...especially when they were wrapped around his hips.

'As I understand it, the house was custom-built about four years ago,' Willa was saying.

Intrigued, Rob slung the towel around his neck and pushed his shoulder into the doorframe. Willa hadn't mentioned that she had an appointment this morning and he was surprised to find himself vaguely irked about that. Why hadn't she told him? What was she planning? Why were these men in her house?

The older gentleman saw Rob leaning against the doorframe and lifted his head in acknowledgement. Willa turned, sent him a *go-away* smile and walked over to the wooden and glass doors that led onto the veranda.

'Let me show you the outdoor entertainment area and the garden—and obviously the view.'

Rob lifted his eyebrows at her unsubtle dismissal and wondered whether they were potential buyers. Her divorce would be final in a couple of weeks and the transfer of property should be a simple process, allowing her to dispose of the house as she saw fit.

Rob thought she was mad... The house was incredible, and she'd never be able to afford another property in such an exclusive area again. The views were awesome, and it only needed new furniture and decent art and it would be a fabulous family home...

Except that Willa didn't have a family. And it was ridiculously big for one or even two people. But she would have a family one day... Rob rubbed the back of his neck as he headed to the kitchen for some water. Why the hell was he thinking of Willa and her future family? And why was he irked at the thought of not being a founding member of that family?

He was a short-term option; he could *only* be a short-term option—nothing else.

The doorbell chimed and Rob cursed softly. It was like Grand-damn-Central Station around here this morning. He walked back into the lobby and yanked the front door open.

A fit-looking guy who looked to be a little older than him flashed a confident smile. 'Hey, I'm from Pearson's, the valuers.'

'Yeah? So?'

'Ms Moore here? I've come to do an evaluation on the gym equipment.'

Rob had hardly had any time to process that statement when he saw a thin blonde woman, older than him, walking up the driveway, the ubiquitous tablet in her hand. When she reached the steps she stopped and looked at Rob in approval. He felt like a prime roast in the supermarket, scared that she would pick him up and take him home...

'Well, hello. Who are *you*?' she drawled, her eyes on his bare abs.

For the first time in...well, for ever, he understood why women complained when men had conversations with a woman's chest.

'Who are *you*?' Rob shot back, thoroughly out of sorts and feeling a little left out. Oh, he knew it was childish, but why hadn't Willa discussed this with him?

The cougar introduced herself and laid a hand on his arm. 'I'm here to value the art and the furniture.' She looked past him and gasped.

Rob turned to see that she was gushing over the massive abstract on the wall—the one that both he and Willa hated with a passion.

'Oh, my Gawd, is that a Johnno Davies? Holy mackerel, it *is*!'

'Looks like someone vomited green paint all over a canvas,' Mr Gym Valuer said in a low voice to Rob.

His type of guy, Rob thought. 'It so does.'

He stepped back so that Willa's guests could enter the hall. He gestured to the couch along the opposite side of the wall.

'Take a seat. Willa is busy with…someone else, but I'll let her know that you are here.'

Rob left them in the hall and headed into the kitchen, picking up his mobile from the counter, where it was charging, and firing Willa off a text message.

More people in your hall. What the hell are you doing? And I thought that I was buying your gym equipment!

He growled when he saw that her response was just the thumbs-up icon.

CHAPTER TEN

'YOU'RE LATE.'

Willa, walking into her study two hours later, frowned at his growly words and thundercloud face. Rob was sitting behind her desk and working on her laptop—in her house. Something was wrong with this picture, she thought.

Her desk, *her* laptop, *her* spreadsheets.

'Excuse me?' she said, giving him the opportunity to choose another greeting...to have a do-over.

'Last time I checked you were employed as my accountant, and I've been sitting here twiddling my thumbs waiting for you.'

Willa placed her hand on the back of the chair and looked at the grizzly bear who was occupying her space. Hmm, she didn't need this nonsense, this snarky attitude today.

'Might I remind you that I sat up for most of the night working through that franchise contract that you tossed my way yesterday afternoon? The one you said you needed to send off first thing this morning?'

The muscle in his cheek jumped and his eye twitched. 'That was business.'

'And those people today were *my* business. My world doesn't stop just because you're paying me.' Willa tipped her head. 'Oh, wait. *Are* you paying me? We never actually discussed my salary.'

Rob had the grace to look momentarily ashamed. 'Of course I'm bloody paying you. I just haven't got around to setting that up...' Rob twisted his lips. 'What's your hourly rate?'

Willa remembered the rate she'd seen in one of those advertisements for an accountant and, because she was irritated with him, doubled it.

Rob winced and then nodded. 'Okay.'

Hot damn. Okay, then.

Willa grabbed a pen and notepad and scribbled her bank account details down, before slapping the paper on the desk in front of him. 'And for the use of my home as your office? And my laptop and internet connection?'

He shoved his chair away from the desk and stood up, every inch of him masculine, powerful and angry. 'Why don't you give me an invoice for all the expenses you've incurred on my behalf and I'll do you a transfer right now?'

Willa flashed him a smile, nipped past him and sat in her chair, sighing at the heat in the fabric created by his delicious rear end. 'Okey-dokey—will do.'

Rob shoved his hands into the pockets of his chinos and scowled. 'Why are you acting like this?'

'Why did you change the formula on this spreadsheet? Don't mess with my numbers, dammit!' Willa lifted her eyes from her screen as his question made sense. 'Acting like what?'

'Acting weird.'

Willa's look suggested that he find another way to phrase that question and Rob took the hint. 'These last few days... You're different...'

'Different how?' Willa leaned back in her chair and placed her feet, encased in two-inch scarlet heels, on the corner of the desk, unaware that her skirt had ridden up and he could see most of her thigh.

'Assertive and...bossy. *And* you took the initiative in bed last night...'

Willa smiled slowly. 'You were moaning and panting and groaning... I thought you liked what I did.'

'I did...' Rob expelled his breath on an audible sigh,

looked frustrated and pinned her with hot eyes. 'But we're not allowed to talk about sex in this room, remember? So... Who were those people who were here?' he asked, suddenly changing the subject.

'Property, gym equipment art and furniture valuers.'

'*I* made you an offer on the gym equipment,' Rob pointed out.

'And it was a fair offer, apparently. But I didn't know that until I got an independent valuer in to tell me,' Willa explained.

She'd never believed for one minute that Rob would cheat her—if anything she'd thought that he might over-pay because he felt sorry for her. But this way, having a second opinion, had made her feel loads better. She also had a ball park figure for what she might expect for the modern minimalistic furniture and the awful art—which was a lot, *lot* more than she'd expected.

When she received their written quotes she would put their lowest estimates into a spreadsheet and work out her personal assets and liabilities, and from there she could make informed decisions.

Her decisions. About *her* life—financial and otherwise.

'Why didn't you tell me they were coming? That this was what you were going to do?'

Willa scratched her neck. So *that* was the bug that had climbed up Rob's ass and started chomping on it. He was annoyed because she hadn't asked his opinion or advice.

'Should I have? Was I expected to?' she asked quietly.

'I...well...yeah,' Rob replied. 'We're practically living together!'

'So? In a couple of weeks...a month...we *won't* be living together. You'll be onto your next short-term fling—' Willa kept her voice cool while her heart spluttered at that thought '—and I'll still be making my own decisions. So what's the point?'

'The point is—'

Willa lifted her eyebrows, waiting for him to finish his sentence.

When he didn't, Willa dropped her legs and leaned forward. 'Rob, you told me that this is a no-strings-attached fling. I'm just playing by the rules, and according to those rules you don't get to be huffy when they change. Do you *want* to change any of those rules?'

Rob, his eyes hot and frustrated on hers, took a long time to answer. 'No.'

Willa rested her folded arms on her desk and looked him in the eye. 'Your turn to ask me.'

'Ask me what?'

'Whether I want to change the rules,' Willa explained patiently.

Dear Lord, boys were bad at this give-and-take stuff.

When Rob didn't answer her, she gave him the stink-eye. 'Or don't I get to have a say in this situation? Am I just supposed to be grateful for what you give me and ignore what I want? What I'm feeling?'

'It would be...easier for me,' Rob admitted, honest as usual.

Except that she was no longer in the business of making decisions based on what was easier for other people. She'd been there—been the dumb girl in the wet T-shirt competition that had been her life.

She wasn't doing that any more.

Willa just held Rob's eyes, and he eventually sighed and said, in a resigned tone, 'I know that I'm going to regret not ending this conversation right here and now but...okay. What do *you* want, Willa?'

Willa rolled her eyes. 'There you go again.'

'Are you going to tell me what's bugging you or do I have to guess?' Rob demanded.

Willa could see that he was fast running out of patience. If she was going to do this, it was now or never.

Doormat Willa lifted up her head to whisper, *Preferably never...*

Willa took a deep breath. 'I want to change the rules... about us.'

'Meaning?'

Willa swallowed. 'Meaning that I don't just want an affair with you any more. Meaning that I want this to mean something, to go somewhere—to be more than me working for you and sleeping with you.'

Rob sat up, placed his forearms on his thighs and looked at her across the desk. He swore softly. 'Dammit, Willa, we weren't going to do this.'

'I can't help the way I feel,' Willa said. 'And I'm feeling more than I should.'

'I think you're confused. A lot has happened over a month.' Rob rubbed his jaw with his hand. 'We met, fell into bed, you got the job, you met your old friends... It's been a busy month. You're...'

Willa lifted her eyebrows in irritation. 'I'm...what?'

'Overwhelmed...you're overwhelmed.'

And wasn't *that* a verbal pat on the head? *God!* Willa looked at her desk and wondered if she could risk braining him with her stapler. It was big and heavy, and she only wanted to bash some sense into him, not kill him.

'I'm *overwhelmed*. Ah, now I understand.' She spoke softly. 'Thanks for clearing it up for me.'

'I hate your sarky quiet voice.'

'You once said you loved it,' Willa pointed out.

'Not when its directed at *me!*' Rob glared at her. 'God, where is this coming from? I don't recognise you any more!'

Willa felt her blood snap and crackle with temper. 'You mean you don't recognise the quiet, meek woman who asked *How high?* and *How far?* when you asked her to jump? You don't recognise this one, who can make her own decisions, who knows her own soul, who doesn't need your protection, your big badass attitude to keep her from harm?' Willa shouted. 'You talk a good talk about women being equal and strong and standing up for themselves, but you can't walk the walk!'

'That's not fair—'

'Isn't it?' Willa demanded as all her old insecurities bubbled to the surface. 'You wanted a one-night stand; I gave it to you. You wanted an affair: I said yes. You wanted to move in after Wayne was here and I said okay. But you're not happy when I get people in to value my art, my house, my possessions, because I didn't run it past you first. You wanted an accountant and I begged you to hire me—'

'Begged? What?'

'It's all about you. When I say that I want something—something more from you—you think that I'm asking you to handle a vial of Ebola. I'm good enough on your terms, but not for anything more!'

'We *both* agreed on nothing more!' Rob roared as he pushed his chair back so hard that it skittered over the dark shiny floor.

He loomed over her desk and Willa, feeling at a disadvantage, leaped to her feet.

'*You're* the one who is complicating this! I don't *do* complications! I fancy you, I adore your body, I enjoy your friendship and I think you are an excellent accountant—'

'Influenced by the fact that I give you sex at the end of the day,' Willa interrupted with a hot shout.

Rob's eyes hardened. 'That comment isn't worthy of you and it's an insult to me.'

Willa slapped a hand on her heart. 'Dear God, I've insulted you. I'm *so* sorry!' she fake gushed.

Rob raked both hands through his hair. 'Why can't you just take this for what it is? Why are you pushing for more?'

Willa slapped her hands on the desk. 'Because I *deserve* more, dammit! Because I deserve a man who will love me and trust me, who wants to be with me, who wants to complicate the hell out of his life *because* of me.'

Rob, his chest heaving, stared at her for a long time before slowly shaking his head. 'I'm not that man, Willa. I said I could never be that man. I've always been honest with you.'

Willa stepped back and folded her arms as her temper drained away. 'Okay, then. But I am not prepared to settle for less than I deserve.'

Rob looked astounded for a second, before his I-don't-care expression slid back into place. 'You're breaking it off?'

'Yes.'

'You're sure you want to do that? I don't go back…*ever*.'

Willa wanted to hyperventilate. This was a big step—a huge step…an irrevocable step. Was her self-respect worth it? Was not having more of Rob worth the pain of not having any of Rob? Was she just acting out of anger? Fear?

You deserve more…you deserve it all.

She did. She really did. She was no longer prepared to settle for the crumbs of life. She wanted the meat and potatoes *and* the sushi *and* the tiramisu of life. She wanted it all.

She sucked in a breath and nodded her head. 'The only thing I'm sure of is that I want more than this.'

Rob swore softly, stood up straight and jammed his hands in his pockets. A stranger took the place of her lover and she wanted to weep.

'And your job?' he asked.

Ah, her job. 'As you said, the one has nothing to do with the other. I'll carry on for as long as you need me.'

'That might not be for much longer,' Rob stated, his voice cool and his expression remote. 'Patrick will be back to work in a couple of weeks or so and he'll take over. However, I do need to go home anyway. We can correspond via email—at a push by phone.'

Behind her back Willa linked her hands, squeezing them so that she kept her tears at bay. This was it. He was walking out of her life and it was the most dreadful experience...*ever.*

Rob gestured to the door. 'I'll just go and pack my stuff.'

'Some of your clothes are in the laundry.' Willa managed to get the words out. 'Just lock the door when you leave.'

Taking my heart with you...

Rob flung his clothes into a duffel bag before stomping to the bathroom and, with one swipe, dropping his toiletries into the bag as well. What the hell had just happened? One moment he was irritated that Willa hadn't spoken to him about the valuers coming round and the next he was being booted out through the door like a bad smell.

And what was all that about it all being his way? He didn't understand this...*any* of this.

Except that wasn't true, he thought, sitting down on the bed where they had spent so much time laughing and loving and being together. For the first time in his life he'd tumbled into a woman's arms, into her life and world, and forgotten to put up barriers to keep her out and to keep his emotions tightly corralled.

He'd allowed them a little bit of freedom and in the process had totally forgotten that freedom always came with a price.

'I want more than this.'

He didn't have more to give her—he *couldn't.* He had responsibilities back home, a life he'd worked very hard to establish. He didn't want to let her go but he couldn't give her anything more than what they currently had.

Rob rubbed his hand over his face. Yes, he was establishing his company in Australia, but that didn't mean he'd be in the country for any length of time in the future; managers would be hired and he'd only be around occasionally.

Willa wouldn't settle for a man who dropped in and out of her life. She couldn't be his priority and she was right: she deserved to be. She deserved a man who could give his whole heart—someone who was willing to love her and be loved in return…someone who knew how to trust, to try.

Rob rubbed at his chest above his heart. It felt as if it was being put through a mincemeat machine.

Feeling ridiculous, he hauled in a deep breath. It was just a short fling, he told himself, happy for the first time ever to lie. There was nothing to feel hurt about. She'd just blindsided him with her talk of wanting more. He didn't do more—never had, never would. It was better that they were calling this quits now, before they got in too deep and too far and someone got hurt.

She'd asked, he'd answered, and now they were done.

Except that he didn't feel as if he was done…as if it was over. He wasn't quite sure how he was going to manage walking out of her door, out of her life.

His heart wanted to stay yet his brain insisted he go. And he always, *always* listened to his brain.

His heart was too vulnerable to make decisions like these.

A week later Willa's divorce, which she'd all but forgotten about, was finally granted. Kate, refusing to let her slink back to her house to lick her very wounded heart alone, dragged her off to Saints, where Amy and Jessica waited at a secluded table in the corner of the Surry Hills restaurant.

After accepting their hugs and congratulations on having The Pain officially removed from her life, Willa slipped into a chair and couldn't help the tears that slid down her face.

'Oh, dear God,' Amy said, grabbing her serviette and trying to dab Willa's eyes from across the table.

'Why are you crying?' Jessica demanded. 'I thought you *wanted* to get divorced?'

Kate smacked Jessica's hand with the back of a spoon. 'It's stress relief. It's a fairly natural reaction; I see it all the time.'

As if she would waste any of her tears on Wayne-the-Pain, Willa scoffed. He wasn't worth it. No, she didn't care about Wayne, or her divorce, or anything to do with her past.

Except Rob. That was the only part of her past she regretted. That she wanted back. Who would ever have thought she could miss someone she'd only known for a month so much? Her heart ached from morning to night and her house had never seemed bigger or emptier or lonelier before. Her fridge was empty, she'd made quite a dent in the contents of the wine cellar, and she spent hours looking out to sea, reliving her too-short time with him.

One minute she was cursing herself for not taking every minute he could give her, and then she felt that she'd done the right thing—that she'd been right to ask for more. She loved him, but she knew that he wasn't obligated to love her back. That wasn't in the rulebook of life.

These feelings would fade, she realised. The hurt and the despair would go away eventually. But his memory never would.

Another batch of fat tears rolled down her face.

'Hey,' Kate murmured, putting her arm around Willa. 'It'll be okay, honey. Let's get some cocktails into you and dry up your tears... Didn't you tell me that you and Rob were going to do something wild to celebrate your divorce?'

'If he was here... He's left.'

Three sets of eyes locked on to her face.

Willa sniffed, wiped her eyes and lifted her shoulders. 'It's over. He went back to South Africa a week ago.'

'Why didn't you call me?' Kate demanded.

'Or me?' Amy added.

Because she'd needed to be alone. Because she was used to being alone. Her friends would have come running, bringing ice cream and sympathy.

She'd done them a disservice, Willa realised. If they asked her for help she'd give it without hesitation...why did she assume they wouldn't?

'I'm sorry; I didn't think. I should've called you...'

Kate leaned forward. 'Are you *sort of* over or *over* over?'

'And why?' Jessica demanded.

Willa wondered how to answer that, and eventually decided she was too tired and too sad to sugar-coat the truth. Maybe Rob's honesty had rubbed off on her.

'There are a couple of reasons—the big one being that I am in love with him and I want more. And he doesn't. I'm tired of being in relationships that work for the men in my life and not for me. And Rob had it great—he had an accountant on tap, and when he was done with her he had a lover. All very nice and easy and uncomplicated.'

Amy looked from Willa to Kate and back to Willa. 'I understand the bit about you want more and he doesn't, but what are you on about with regard to your job?'

Willa shrugged. 'He needed someone to do the work. I was handy. It wasn't like he interviewed anyone else...he took the easy way out.'

'Willa, don't you remember how hard you fought him to get that job?' Amy cried, exasperated. 'It would have been a hell of a lot easier for him to hire an accountant with experience, and with no messy personal ties.'

'Not to mention cheaper,' Kate commented, her chin in the palm of her hand.

Willa frowned. 'What?'

'Do you remember that discussion we had about your future? I asked you about what income you could expect? You told me what rate Rob was paying you and I was slightly irked because it was more than *my* hourly rate. Then I looked it up and it's more than double what experienced CPAs are getting.'

Amy grinned, and Willa knew that she wasn't picking up the point Kate was trying to make. 'I don't understand what you're trying to say.'

'She's saying that Rob would never pay anybody double the going rate if he didn't think they were worth it,' Jessica stated.

'Not even *you* are that good, honey.' Kate patted her arm.

Willa's mouth opened and shut like a fish. 'But—'

'But what?' Amy demanded. 'Willa, how did you manage to forget that Rob is the most honest, direct, man you've ever met? Hell, *we've* ever met!'

'Um…'

'If he employed you, he thought you were worth that money. If he was with you, it was because he wanted to be with you. His honesty would demand nothing less,' Amy raged on. 'He could have just walked on out after that first night, but he didn't—he stuck around.'

'Um, I—'

'If you told him you loved him and he didn't return that love then that's one thing,' Kate added. 'But you can't accuse him of not being honest, Willa, of having ulterior motives.'

Willa looked past Jessica but didn't see the customers in the packed restaurant. She just saw Rob's face…confusion, hurt and panic in his eyes.

'I didn't actually tell him that I loved him.'

Amy dropped her face into her serviette and groaned. Willa thought she heard a muffled swear-word. 'This just gets worse and worse.'

'I just said that I needed more. He said not to complicate things and I ended it.'

Kate took a big sip from the glass of wine at her elbow.

'Dear God in heaven—you shouldn't be allowed out on your own. You said you wanted *more*…what does he think "more" means? Marriage? Living together? Donating a kidney?'

'Nothing like that. I just want to be with him—be able to know that he is mine, and I'm his…that we can give this… *thing* between us a chance,' Willa protested.

'Boys need to be told carefully and in short sentences, using small words, what you want,' Jessica told her, her face serious. 'Like Winnie-the-Pooh, big words baffle them, and an open-ended statement like "I want more" sends them into a tailspin.'

'Especially men who are as commitment-phobic and distrustful as Rob,' Amy added.

Willa sighed. 'Maybe I should give up on men and get me to a nunnery.'

'And never have any fantastic sex again? *Pfft*…' Kate muttered.

Willa cocked her head, happy to move the spotlight off her. 'Are you having fantastic sex that I don't know about?'

'Only with Big Burt—and his batteries are flat.' Kate sighed. 'I keep forgetting to replace the damn things.'

Jessica's eyes widened. 'Why would anyone name their vibrator Burt?'

'*From Here to Eternity*…Burt Lancaster?'

Jessica looked blank and Kate rolled her eyes. 'Seriously? You've never heard of either the film or the star?'

'As fascinating as your sex-life is or isn't…' Amy smiled at Kate but refused to be distracted '…we're talking about Willa and the utter cock-up she's made of her life.'

'Just for a change…' Willa murmured.

'Stop whining,' Amy said sharply.

Willa heard Rob's voice saying the same thing. Okay, no whining—even though she felt as if her life was falling apart.

'And tell me what you are going to do about Rob. And if you say *nothing*, I swear I will stab you with my butter knife.'

What *could* she do about Rob? Willa thought later that night, sitting at her desk in the study, the night inky black behind her. What did she *want* to do? What did she *want* from him?

Marriage? Kids? Fifty years of sharing beds and bathrooms and domesticity? Did she want to be someone's wife again? She'd just become Willa again, and she didn't think she was ready for such a drastic step—with Rob or anyone.

So what *was* she ready for? What did she *know*?

She knew that she missed Rob—that every day without him, instead of getting easier, just became more difficult. She knew that her house, when he was in it, became a home and not a collection of expensively furnished rooms.

Rob being gone was confirmation that she definitely didn't need a gentle man, as he'd once said. She didn't need someone to ease her into life again. She needed Rob's unflinching honesty, his way of making her see her surroundings and herself clearly. And maybe her friends were right—maybe she had been stupid to question his desire to be with her, to spend time with her. Rob, honest to the core, wouldn't do anything he didn't want to.

When he'd been with her it had been because he was exactly where he'd wanted to be. Even if it was as a temporary fling...for an affair that had an expiration date. He'd never promised or even suggested more...

It wasn't *his* fault that she wanted more than they'd had. She wanted love, obviously. And fidelity. And a level of commitment—not necessarily marriage. But mostly she just wanted him.

Gruff, honest, direct. Full of integrity.

And she wanted him to trust her. With his business, his

heart, his love, his life. That was non-negotiable—the line in the sand. She knew what it was like to live with a man who didn't respect her, didn't include her, who thought of her as a possession and not with pride. She wanted to be a fully invested partner in every way possible.

But to be that Rob would need to trust her. The one thing he couldn't do.

Willa leaned back in her chair and propped her bare feet on the desk. She couldn't accuse him of deceiving her... the opposite was true. Rob had always treated her fairly, with honesty. From the first time she'd suggested they sleep with each other he'd told her that they couldn't have anything but good sex. She was just a way to pass the time while he was in Oz. Then she'd said that she wanted more, and he'd said no.

Honest, direct, final.

Willa placed her forearm over her eyes and sighed. *But if you could make him change his mind, universe, that would be great.*

Any time you want to.

CHAPTER ELEVEN

BACK HOME IN Johannesburg, Rob was in the pool, two feminine arms looped around his shoulders and an exquisite face buried in the crook of his neck. He smiled when he heard low chuckles as his fingers tickled her ribcage.

Little Kiley, her chubby legs kicking against the water and narrowly missing his crotch, squirmed in his arms and he let her drop into the water. She fell like a stone and popped up a couple of seconds later, laughing. At four, Kiley was a fish, and she loved the water as much as he did.

Her hand clutched his arm and he looked down into her face, thinking that he'd like a little girl one day—or a little boy with greeny-silver eyes and dark hair, Willa's stubborn chin...

Not going there...

To distract himself he looked around and saw that his mum, on the veranda, was putting the last platter of food on the long wooden table and his Uncle Sid was taking a seat at the head of it.

'Grub's up,' he told his family.

Patrick was lying on a double lounger next to his wife Heather, under an umbrella at the shallow end of the pool, and his sister Gail was snuggled up in the colourful arms of the tattoo artist playing tonsil tennis.

Gack.

'Cut it out before I turn a hose on you two,' he called, and ignored Gail's rolling eyes when she surfaced for air. If he wasn't getting kissed then nobody else should be either.

Especially his baby sister, who surely wasn't old enough to be kissed like that!

Rob boosted Kiley out of the pool and climbed out himself, reaching for a towel and wrapping it around his hips. Pulling on a T-shirt, he walked towards the veranda and took the beer Sid held out to him.

It was a stunning day, and the people he cared most about, the ones he loved and trusted, were all here. All but one…

How weird that he felt that his group, his family, was missing an important element… Willa wasn't here and his family didn't feel complete.

Rob pulled out a chair and tried to ignore his feeling of discontent. It was what it was, he told himself. Nothing had changed…

He smiled as Kiley climbed up onto his lap, blithely ignoring the booster chair her father was urging her into.

'Hey, I'm your *dad*,' Patrick complained good-naturedly.

'But I'm her favourite person,' Rob replied as she wound her arms around his neck.

'Only because you bring her presents and sneak her ice cream when we're not looking.'

'Godparent privilege.'

'Bribery,' Patrick shot back, sitting down next to him. '*Now* I understand your success rate with women.'

Rob's smile was a bit forced. 'Heather's looking a lot better,' he said, changing the subject.

Rob pushed his hair back from his face as Kiley pretended his thigh was a horse, waiting impatiently for Heather to dish her up some food. God, he missed Willa—wanted her here. He'd never missed any of his short-term flings before; normally he wished them well and seldom thought of again. Not the case with Willa, who was the first thing he thought of in the morning and the last thought he had at night. Then he dreamed about her—hot, *hot*, sensual dreams that woke him up with a hard-on from hell.

Such fun. *Not*.

'I deserve a man who will love me and trust me, who wants to be with me, who wants to complicate the hell out of his life because of me.'

He wanted to be that man. It was that simple and that complicated. Yet he couldn't be that man...

Gail and Tattoo sat opposite him and immediately leaned towards each other for another kiss.

'Give it a rest, for God's sake,' he muttered, and Gail, the witch, just laughed.

When they all had plates piled high in front of them, Gail leaned back in her chair and pushed her hair off her forehead. 'I have an announcement to make.'

Rob, his fork halfway to his mouth, gave her a hard stare. A sentence starting with those words could never be good. He lowered his fork and took a sip of his beer, his eyes not leaving his sister's face. Whatever she was thinking about doing, she could just forget it. She was *not* moving in with or marrying Tattoo, and if she said she was pregnant or that she was quitting uni he'd freak.

'As you all know, I'll be receiving my degree in three months.'

No, that wasn't possible. She hadn't been at university that long, Rob thought. Mentally rewinding, he realised that she had and wondered where the time had gone.

'I've decided to take a gap year,' Gail said, her voice serious. 'I'm going to London for a couple of months and then I'm going to travel.'

Oh, hell, no. How could he look after her if she was bouncing all over the world?

Rob shook his head. 'No, you're not.'

His mum leaned across Patrick to place a hand on his

forearm. 'Yeah, honey, she is.' Her voice was soft but determined, and it brooked no argument. 'I'm her parent, not you, and she has my full support.'

Gail sent him a mischievous look. 'Yeah, I'm cutting the umbilical cord. Jumping the nest. Spreading my—'

Rob held up his hand for her to be quiet. It didn't work. 'Spreading my wings. Flying the coop.'

Their mum's piercing look stopped Gail's crowing. 'I'm asking Rob to step away, but *I'm* still going to keep a very sharp eye on you, young lady. You have the impulse control of a two-year-old.'

Rob felt as if he'd dropped into a black hole. What was happening? He had to get this conversation—his life—back on track.

He placed his beer bottle on the table and folded his arms against his chest. 'Can we talk about this? It's a pretty big decision. We *need* to talk about this!'

Okay, that hadn't come out right. He'd sounded panicky and stressed and...*unhinged*.

His mum shook her head and he immediately recognised her stubborn expression. 'Talking about it won't change anything; she *is* going. You have to trust her—and me—enough to step away and let us deal with this. And while we're on the subject you need to stop mollycoddling us, darling. Enough now, okay?'

Rob knew that his mouth was open and that he was trying to speak, but no words were coming out. Taking his silence for permission, or acceptance, his family started a lively discussion about their plans for the future. A future he had no control over.

'You have to trust her—and me... Stop mollycoddling us.' Could he? Could he do that? He didn't think so. Standing guard over them had become a habit and...a shield. An excuse...

After a couple of minutes Patrick nudged him with his shoulder. 'So, *that* was a mighty kick up the jack, wasn't it?'

Rob turned to look at him, not realising that his eyes held fear and hope. And relief.

'Guess they just handed you a Get Out of Jail Free card, dude.'

'I have no idea what you are talking about,' Rob muttered.

Patrick chuckled, enjoying his cousin's predicament a little too much. 'Please… Everyone realises that you're trying to atone for leaving them with Stefan by hovering over them. But what you've never understood is that nobody ever blamed you for that…except you.' He grinned. 'And that's because you're an idiot. Now you have no excuse not to get your ass on the first plane out and go to Willa.'

Yes. No. Hell, maybe.

Rob stared down at his plate and lifted his broad shoulders. 'I hurt her, cuz.'

As a reasonable adult, and his best friend, Rob expected Patrick's support—a statement of wisdom, of thoughtful consideration. Instead Patrick just shook his head and placed his hand on his daughter's back.

'Kiley, honey?'

Kiley lifted her mouth from gnawing on a chicken bone to look his way. 'Mmmph?'

'What do we do when we do something bad or naughty?' Patrick asked in a gentle voice.

'Say sorry,' Kiley muttered, her mouth full of chicken.

Patrick's eyes laughed at Rob. 'See—even my four-year-old has a better handle on the situation than you,' he stated.

Rob narrowed his eyes at his cousin, his expression promising retribution. 'You think you are so damn smart, don't you?' He growled the words.

Patrick clinked his beer bottle against Rob's and shrugged. 'Nah, I don't think I am—I *know* I am.'

* * *

Willa, coming in from her morning run, heard her mobile ringing from where she'd left it on the hall table and fumbled her key into the lock of the front door. Thinking, hoping that it might be Rob, she barrelled through the door and snatched the phone up with a raspy, breathless, 'Hello?'

'Is that Willa Moore?'

Not Rob. Damn.

She almost replied that she was Willa Fisher-Moore, then remembered at the last minute that she was divorced and that she was reverting to her maiden name. 'Yes. Can I help you?'

'Hopefully.'

The caller gave his name and his company's name and Willa wrote them down on a notepad on the hall table. She'd heard of the company—a vitamin distribution company—and wondered why the CFO was calling her.

'Rob Hanson gave me your name. We're working together on a deal to supply his stores with our brand of supplements.'

'Okay...' Willa perched her bum on the edge of the hall table.

'In conversation, when he was raving about his superbright and intuitive Australian accountant, he told me how you'd found a creative way to work around an issue with foreign-owned entities.'

Say what? 'Please go on,' Willa said.

'Well, we have an issue that we have to solve before we launch our company on the Stock Exchange and we've had a dozen accountants look at it and tell us its irresolvable. Rob suggested that you take a look and that if *you* can't find a way around it then it *is* impossible. He said that you are bright and brilliant and that he'd trust you with his life.'

Willa felt the warm liquid rush of pleasure. God, could anything be sexier than an endorsement of her brain and her skills? Oh, she knew that Rob loved her body, but this... this was the best gift he could have given her.

Apart from his love and a happy-ever-after, obviously.

'Ms Moore?'

Willa pulled herself back to the conversation. 'I won't do anything illegal or immoral, but if you'd like to e-mail me your sticky problem I'll take a look. No guarantees, though.'

'Understood. I'm just grateful that you'll look at it. Obviously we'll compensate you for the hours you spend on it.'

Willa gave him her details, her hourly rate and her e-mail address, and when she'd ended the call held her mobile to her chest.

If she'd been see-sawing between love and lust this one action would have tipped her into love. Acceptance, validation, pride... By recommending her to his business cohorts he'd shown her that he knew she wouldn't let him down, that he was confident in her abilities, maybe that he trusted her a little. In business, at least.

If only he could trust her with his heart and his love and his time.

Universe...again? Please?

Rob turned off the ignition of his hired car and swallowed at the 'For Sale' sign hammered into the grass next to the kerb. So Willa had decided to sell. A pity, because he loved this house. Loved the view, loved the openness...the access to the bay.

In a perfect world he could see him and Willa sharing their time between this house and his house in Jo'burg, with frequent visits to the family beach cottage in Knysna. If they had kids one day then they would have to settle down somewhere, maybe in Sydney, but really it didn't matter where. Being together was important. Houses and things not so much.

But he wasn't living in a perfect world. He was currently inhabiting a twilight world where nothing really made sense. Until he spoke to Willa and knew what course his future was taking then nothing would.

Heaven or hell. He would be experiencing one or the other fairly soon.

Rob pulled his keys out of the ignition and stepped out of the vehicle, his heart pounding in his chest. He walked up to the front door and thought about ringing the doorbell, but after all they'd shared that just made him feel stupid. Instead he tried the door, and—what a surprise—it opened to his touch.

Willa! God, how was he *ever* going to get her to take security seriously?

The first thing he noticed when he stepped into the hall was that the abstract painting on the wall was gone—and good riddance. Johnno Davies was one of the most famous artists around, but Rob didn't care what anyone said—green streaks on a white canvas could never be masterpiece.

Rob glanced at his watch; it was seven thirty and he wondered where she was. In the library-cum-office, working—Patrick kept tossing more work her way—or in the TV lounge? In bed reading?

In bed with someone else?

The thought popped into his head and his blood froze. *No damn way.*

Sprinting up to her bedroom, he flung her bedroom door open and found Willa on the bed, dressed in denim shorts and a sleeveless top, painting her toenails a fiery red. No lover to beat to a pulp.

At the sight of an intruder, Willa let out a blood-curdling scream.

A few moments later she felt her heart settle in her ribcage, slowed down her breathing and felt as if her world was realigning itself on its axis. He wasn't a murderer, he was Rob, and the cosmos was falling into sync again.

Unless he was here to tell her that there wasn't a chance in hell that they would ever be together?

Oh, hell...her heart had started bouncing again.

She made herself speak past whatever was blocking her throat. 'Um...why are you here?'

'Are you alone?' he demanded, his hands on his hips and looking fierce.

'Apart from the male strippers in my bathroom...'

Rob didn't look even vaguely amused at her quip, so she sighed and waved the nail polish brush around, not realising that she was flecking her white bed linen with red.

'Of course I'm alone.' Willa tacked an implied *moron* onto the end of that sentence.

Rob walked around the bed, took the nail polish from her and replaced the cap. Tossing it into the bedside drawer, he retreated a couple of steps and jammed his hands into the pockets of his Levi's, his eyes hooded...and wild.

Willa ignored the fact that only a couple of toes were painted and wrapped her arms around her knees, not having the foggiest idea what to say. She'd already asked once why he was here—should she ask again?

'Why—?'

'I—'

Their words collided and they both stopped speaking. Willa lifted her hands in a gesture for him to carry on talking.

'I want to change the rules,' he said, shocking her to the core.

Willa could hardly hear her own cool voice over the roaring in her ears. What did he mean? What *could* he mean? '*You* want to change them this time?'

A muscle ticked in Rob's jaw. 'Yeah. I want to totally rewrite them, in fact.'

'Ah. Um…'

Okay, it was official. He'd turned her into a blathering idiot. She swallowed, gripped her knees harder to keep them from knocking, and searched his face for a clue. It was there in the vulnerability in his eyes, in the tremor in his normally confident voice.

'I'm going to need a bit more of an explanation, here, Rob.'

Rob shoved his hand into his curls and tugged. 'I was at home and my family were all there but you weren't. The most important part of my family was missing and it didn't make any sense.'

Oh… Oh. Oh, my…Willa felt tears shimmer in her eyes as her mind started filling with possibilities. Did she dare hope?

'I missed you every minute,' Rob said, his voice hoarse.

'Me too.'

Rob kept his hands firmly in his pockets and Willa wished she could touch him, feel his heat, his hard body. But she knew that if they touched right now they would fall into lust and passion when they needed to talk through the emotion shimmering between them.

'I really meant it to be a fling, but you crawled under my skin and into my heart. You're smart and brave and wonderful and I—'

Willa held her breath.

'And I think that I'm in love with you.' Rob held up his hand as a delighted smile crossed her face. 'I've never been in love before, so I could be wrong.'

'Me neither.' Willa pulled a face when he looked sceptical. 'I haven't… Not as an adult with her eyes wide open.'

A smile finally touched the corners of Rob's mouth. 'So, what does love feel like?'

Willa tipped her head back to look at him, her face and her tone serious. 'It feels likes home—like my life suddenly makes sense with you in the room. It feels soft, but strong. I'm ecstatic that you're back and so, so grateful that you are. It feels…perfect.'

Rob just stared at her, a mix of naked emotion, hope and lust on his face.

Stepping towards her, he sat on the edge of the bed and lifted his hand to her face. 'It does feel perfect.' His thumb brushed her cheekbone.

'Missed you…' she murmured softly.

Rob groaned as his forehead touched hers. 'Missed you too, honey.'

'Rob?' Willa said, when he just stayed where he was, his body radiating tension.

Why wasn't he kissing her, holding her, ripping her clothes off her? Heat throbbed down below and she thought that if she didn't have his solid weight on her soon she would quite simply spontaneously combust.

'Mmm?'

'Are you going to kiss me some time soon?'

'If I do I'm going to be inside you so damn fast we'll go up in flames,' Rob retorted, licking his lips.

'And why would that be a problem?' Willa asked softly, draping her arms around his neck.

Rob's hand spanned her waist before moving over to her bottom. 'Another example of my idiocy… It's not a problem at all.'

Sex was different when love was involved, Willa thought, watching her naked man leave the bed and head into the bathroom. Always spectacular before, making love—and that was what it now was—was deeper, hotter, more thrilling. Her heart had orgasmed along with her happy place, and it was a feeling that she knew she'd never get enough of.

She wouldn't ever get enough of looking at Rob either—

naked, dressed…it didn't matter. Preferably naked, though, she thought as he walked out of the bathroom back to the bed.

Rob placed his hands on his hips, looked towards the bathroom, and then looked down at her. 'If we're going to be doing this for next fifty decades, at least, can I ask you a favour?'

Willa sat up and leaned back against the leather head-board, her soul singing at his reference to the rest of their lives. There wasn't anything she wouldn't do for him when he looked at her with love in his eyes.

'Sure…what?' she asked as he sat down next to her on the bed, facing her.

'Can you go on the pill? I want to be with you without the feeling of latex.'

Willa blinked at his prosaic statement, and then she laughed. Typical Rob, so damn forthright. 'I can do that. For you.'

'Well, since there won't *be* anyone else for you it had better be for me,' Rob growled, picking up her hand and placing a kiss on her wrist.

'So we are fully monogamous?' Willa asked.

'Hell, yes. Fully monogamous, fully involved, no half-measures.' Rob placed his hands on either side of her hips and leaned forward, his eyes demanding her full attention. 'I was wrong before.'

'For what?' Willa asked. 'For leaving me?'

'That too,' Rob admitted. 'I don't *think* I'm in love with you; I *am* in love with you. You okay with that?'

Willa sighed. 'Very.'

'I'm tough and tactless and honest—'

Willa placed her fingers on his mouth to stop him from talking. 'And you love me. But—'

He frowned. 'But?'

'Do you trust me?'

He swallowed as his eyes filled with emotion. 'I do, I promise. For me, I can't do one without the other.'

'Then that's the biggest gift you can give me. Along with the fact that you love me as I am...that you see me clearly. I love that—and I love you.'

Rob's eyes reflected the emotion that was brimming in hers. 'I never thought I needed to hear the words...hear a woman—*my* woman—speak them. I never realised the power, the...the hope for the future.'

Willa placed her face in the crook of his neck as he gathered her close. Their naked bodies tangled together, arms and legs and bits and bobs all finding their place, settling in, knowing that they were home. Her heart settled and sighed, and her soul curled up next to its warmth.

Willa yawned and Rob gently tugged her head back by her hair, so that he could see her face. 'You haven't been sleeping?'

'No, and neither have you,' Willa replied, before yawning again. 'Let's have a nap and then we'll find something for supper.'

But Rob's hand was cupping her bottom and his hardening erection told her that he had other plans.

'Or we can do that instead,' she said.

Rob pushed her back onto the bed and loomed over her, his erection nudging her entrance. He groaned. 'I just want to *feel* you...'

Willa surged up and he slipped inside, harder and hotter and so much better without a condom.

'Ah...hell...' Rob groaned and pulled out, cursing as he reached for a condom out of the box that lived in the bedside drawer. 'I'm not prepared to risk it. I'm too selfish to share you with a mini-me or mini-you just yet.'

Willa sighed her relief as she helped him roll on a condom. Kids were for the future—not for a while yet. She wanted to be selfish too, and concentrate on loving Rob. And having Rob love her…

As he was doing right now—and incredibly well too.

Much, much later they made it to the kitchen and Willa, feeling as if her legs had turned to Jello, slid onto a stool and placed her arms on the granite counter. She tucked Rob's T-shirt under her bare bottom and thought that Rob had never looked more sexy, wearing jeans and a satisfied, happy smile.

Except that the smile was now replaced with a frown as he pulled his face out of the fridge. 'Didn't you eat while I was gone? There's nothing in here!'

Willa lifted a shoulder. 'What was the point? I couldn't taste anything.'

Rob's eyes softened before he reached back into the fridge and pulled out a carton of eggs and a block of mouldy cheese. After hacking off the mould he beat the eggs and grated the cheese while Willa watched him.

'I'm sorry I hurt you,' he stated quietly. 'It was never my intention.'

'I know,' Willa replied, looking at her hands.

While she knew that she loved him, and he loved her, they still had a lot to work through.

'What now, Rob?'

Rob lifted an eyebrow at her.

'I don't want to push you into a corner, but where do we go from here?' Willa gabbled. 'Are you going to commute? How often will I see you? Can we *do* this?'

Rob reached across the counter and placed his hand on hers and squeezed. 'Willa…relax. We'll work it out… Let's eat first and then we'll chat.'

After polishing off cheese omelettes and toast and marmalade Willa made coffee and they walked onto the veranda to take advantage of the warm night.

Willa went to sit on one of the chairs, but Rob yanked her over to his chair and pulled her down onto his lap.

'I have no intention of letting you be more than a hair's breadth away from me for the foreseeable future.' He placed a kiss on her temple. 'Okay, let's thrash this out. I saw the "For Sale" sign outside—are you wanting to sell this house?'

Willa shrugged. 'It's so big...'

'For one person. For a couple too. But I like the space. It would be a wonderful family home later on.' Rob looked around. 'I'd buy it from you...for us.'

Willa looked at him in astonishment. 'Seriously? You'd live here?'

'In a heartbeat. I'd live in a tin shack if you were in it. But, that aside, if you want the cash in the bank I'll buy it. If you want to keep it as yours—as your asset—and share it with me, that's good too. If you want to sell it, that's your choice,' Rob said. 'I can't live here full-time, Wills. I have to go home regularly. My business needs me there and I like being around my family—even though half of them are going travelling. A long story,' he said at her quizzical look.

'Okay. So I'd see you every couple of months?' Willa swallowed. It wasn't ideal, but...

'Hell, no. Where I go, you go.' Rob twisted his lips as he realised what he'd said. 'That came out wrong. I'm hoping that you will continent-hop with me. Live with me here *and* there.'

Willa thought for a moment and sighed. 'I hate the thought of not being with you, but I do need to work, Rob. I don't want to be idle, useless—like I was. That means finding a job.'

'You *have* a job.'

Rob laughed at her shock.

'And this time it has nothing to do with me. Patrick wants you to carry on working with him... There's too much work and you've been taking a load off his shoulders. He said that even if I was idiotic enough to give you up *he* wasn't going to—you're too valuable to let go. So you'd report to him, not me, and it wouldn't matter if you worked here or there. Both.'

Willa couldn't believe his words and her stomach filled with warmth, with the thrill of knowing that her work was valued. 'That sounds amazing... I'd love to carry on working for...' she grinned at him '...for Patrick.'

Rob just shook his head and brushed his mouth against hers. 'Let me know what you want to do about this house, but the furniture has to go.'

'Okay,' Willa agreed, her head resting on his shoulder. She felt Rob take a deep breath and wondered what he was going to say next.

'Do you want to get married?'

Willa swallowed down the impulsive need to say yes and thought about his question. She could be honest, she reminded herself. Rob could take it.

'I love you, but no...not yet. I just got divorced—a week ago, to be precise—and I want to...*be*. Just be Willa for a while. Can you understand that?'

Rob yawned, and when he sank further down into the chair with her, utterly relaxed, she knew that he was fine with her answer.

'Let me know if that changes,' he said, his arms tightening around her. 'But, married or not, you're mine.'

'I *so* am,' Willa agreed, and allowed her eyes to drift closed.

EPILOGUE

WILLA LAY WITH her head on Rob's shoulder after they'd
spent another day lazing around… AKA spending the day
in bed, getting hot and steamy. It was her absolute favourite way to while away the hours.

Rob's hand stroked her spine and she listened to the re-
assuring thump of his heartbeat under her ear. This was
love, she thought. Quiet, strong, tangible. Willa looked out
of the huge window and sighed at the orange and pink sun-
set… Night was falling and she was starving.

Food…food would be good around about now.

'Rob…?' she wheedled.

She felt his grin. 'No.'

'You don't even know what I was about to ask…'

'Coffee, food, more sex… Actually, yes to more sex.'

She was utterly, crazily, besottedly in love with her man,
but this house was run as a democracy—which meant that
it was his turn to make supper. For about the fourth night
in a row.

'No to everything but the sex,' Rob reiterated.

Willa turned her head and nipped his chest. 'You suck!'
she muttered against his skin.

'No, actually, that was *you*…'

Rob's deep voice drifted over her and she laughed.

'By the way,' he said, 'I had the most amazing day
planned for us today…'

Willa moved back slightly and tipped her head up to look
at his rueful face. 'You did? What? And why?'

'Well, I owe you a day to celebrate your divorce.'

Willa wrinkled her nose, trying to keep up. Then she remembered asking Rob to do something wild with her to celebrate her freedom and she grinned. 'What were we going to do?'

'I hired a Ducati. We were going up the coast for lunch. Then we were booked to go sky-diving or bungee-jumping—and maybe abseiling.'

'Sounds like fun. And what happened to my day?'

Rob rubbed his hand over her butt. 'Well, we started making love and we didn't stop. Your fault.'

'Hey, you made something for me during the night and I had to use it!' Willa protested. 'We'll have to do all that another day...'

'Yeah...'

The strident peal of the doorbell had Willa bolting up in bed, her eyes as wide as saucers.

'The doorbell is ringing...are you expecting anyone?'

Rob looked at his watch. 'Oh, hell, yeah... Sort of forgot about that.'

Willa raised her eyebrows. 'Sort of forgot about what?'

'That would be the cocktail party in your honour.' Rob placed his hands behind his head and looked utterly relaxed. 'Kate and Amy and Jessica are throwing you a we're-so-happy-you're-divorced party.'

Willa placed her hand on her heart and her eyes looked suspiciously moist. 'Aw, that's so sweet. I hope they've organised food and drinks too...'

'Caterers. Hired bar. Hired music.' Rob shrugged.

Willa leaned over him and took his face in her hands. She kissed him before dropping her hands and sliding them over his chest, touching his hard, hot skin. 'I'd much rather call it my so-happy-to-have-found-you party.'

'I like that,' Rob growled.

Willa's fingers danced over his six-pack and slid under the waistband of his briefs.

Rob's eyes deepened with passion and he groaned. 'You keep doing that and we're not going anywhere.'

Willa smirked. 'Works for me.'

Then her mobile vibrated on her nightstand and she leaned across him to pick it up. She grinned and showed him the display with Amy's name on the screen.

Do not make me come and get you. You have fifteen minutes!!!!

Rob grinned and flipped her over. 'There is *so* much that I can do in fifteen minutes.'

He was true to his word—but they were still an hour late for her party.

* * * * *